The Room

The Room

A Novel

Ray Melnik

iUniverse, Inc.
New York Lincoln Shanghai

The Room

iUniverse books may be ordered through booksellers or by contacting:

iUniverse
2021 Pine Lake Road, Suite 100
Lincoln, NE 68512
www.iuniverse.com
1-800-Authors (1-800-288-4677)

Because of the dynamic nature of the Internet, any Web addresses or links contained in this book may have changed since publication and may no longer be valid.

This is a work of fiction. All of the characters, names, incidents, organizations, and dialogue in this novel are either the products of the author's imagination or are used fictitiously.

Book design, cover art and photographs by ntech media design

The novel is set in the small town of Washingtonville, New York, in the lower Hudson Valley. The town stores and people in the novel are fictitious. All other landmarks and locations described in the novel are real.

Beth Quinn's column, referred to in chapter two, does appear on Mondays in the *Times Herald-Record newspaper*, serving New York's Hudson Valley and in the Catskills.

ISBN: 978-0-595-47029-7 (pbk)
ISBN: 978-0-595-70735-5 (cloth)
ISBN: 978-0-595-91313-8 (ebk)

Printed in the United States of America

For Kyle and Leah, my son and daughter
They are my life. My hope is that my generation can
finally learn to take better care of their planet.

Acknowledgments

Special thanks to Edward Hayman for editing, proofreading and enlightening advice.

Additional proofreading by Ira Blutreich

The reference in chapter nine to "how fragile, how breakable we all are" was inspired by the song lyrics to "Breakable" from the "Girls and Boys" CD by Ingrid Michaelson.

To Leonard Susskind for his clear view of reality.

To Brian Greene for his clever illustration of string theory.

Some of the character Harry's views are shaped by the writings of Carl Sagan and Richard Dawkins.

Prologue

Science and philosophy have always asked the questions: "Why do we exist? How did we get here?" Philosophy probes these questions through thought, while science concerns itself with the mechanics of the cosmos. As history fades into the past we look back and know with certainty that many past philosophical ideas are just wrong, just as many theories in science are found to be wrong. But how can we find the answers to our existence without first taking into account all the things we learn about the cosmos? Philosophers like Daniel Dennett, armed with the latest science, are, for me, those on the right path. It's a path that builds on an existentialist view.

Science itself takes a different approach, building on centuries of experience and correcting itself as progress is made. Scientists may search for the same answer in different ways but as the truth is finally revealed, the remaining ideas will be dropped. Science is meant to be self correcting. During the 20th century we saw an explosion in knowledge and it continues today with incredible advances in physics, astronomy, chemistry and biology.

As we ponder our existence, we do a disservice to ourselves when we choose to ignore these discoveries. Still, there are even some with developed intellect who entertain the idea that there may have been an outside force that stirred the quantum pot just right. But the edge of scientific theory moves forward, shattering old barriers along the way. As technology advances, we find ways to test these new theories and put the wrong ideas to bed.

Leonard Susskind is a theoretical physics professor at Stanford University since 1978 and is one of the pioneers of string theory. Scientists like him are not satisfied to attribute the unknown to a conscious all-powerful being. Who created that being? To those who think as Leonard does, that path equates to quitting. If every scientist thought like those who were willing to just give up, what further advancements could we make?

In our place in history we now find ourselves at a new boundary. Once again we find that the mathematics and theories in the field of quantum physics are taking a new leap from our ability to prove them in the lab. But this has happened repeatedly in our history. Many of Einstein's theories had to wait many years before they could be tested.

String theory is one such theory that breaks the current boundary of the ability to test using current technology. But it nonetheless holds great promise in revolutionizing the way we see the cosmos. The excitement is in the hope that we will finally find the theory of everything. The mechanics may soon enough be understood that will link quantum mechanics with Relativity Theory, the very thing that eluded Einstein. After decades of work, physicists working with strings had come up with five different theories. They focused on a cosmos consisting of as many as nine spatial dimensions plus a tenth, time. How could all five theories be right? But the introduction of M-theory revealed that maybe the differences in the five were not differences at all. They could be multiple ways of looking at the same thing. M-theory added one more dimension which brought it to 10 spatial dimensions and one for time, making eleven.

String theory itself portrays a cosmos where all matter and forces consist of vibrating strings of energy. If proven, it seems amazing enough but even more, it opens the possibility of infinite parallel universes.

Brian Greene, author of "The Elegant Universe", a book on string theory, wrote:

> *"And there's no reason to be disappointed with one particular outcome or another, because quantum mechanics suggests that each of the possibilities like getting a yellow juice or a red juice may actually happen. They just happen to happen in universes that are parallel to ours, universes that seem as real to their inhabitants as our universe seems to us.*

Leonard Susskind, in his book, "The Cosmic Landscape," wrote:

> *I am far from the first physicist to seriously entertain the possibility that reality—whatever that means—con-*

tains, in addition to our own world of experience, alter-
nate worlds with different history than our own.

Perhaps one of the most profound realizations is that this theory could finally hold the answer to why our universe is so finely tuned to support life. Infinite parallel universes would mean an infinite amount that would support life and an infinite amount that would not. It would make our universe not so special after all. We are just fortunate enough to be here and because we are here, we question.

It could answer the questions of how and why we are here in a way that's disturbing to those with philosophies that are human centric. But I for one would like to know the truth, no matter where it leads.

I will not delve any deeper into the science but I recommend highly that you read both "The Cosmic Landscape" by Leonard Susskind and "The Elegant Universe" by Brian Greene. They reveal a cosmos far stranger and more exciting than any pseudoscience could ever hope to offer.

In "The Room", I take great liberties in the use of string theory to explain the extraordinary event that engulfs Harry near the end of the book. Many would characterize this event as supernatural, but not Harry. His dedication to science leads him to explore the laws of physics in his attempt to find even a clue.

This event is used in an effort to tell the story about our path in life and how a single decision can determine the course of our future. "The

Room" asks the question: What if parallel universes were true and somehow two of those universes could lightly touch, creating a bubble? In life we must all play the cards we are dealt. But what if in a hand of five, you were dealt ten?

Let me tell you a little about Harry. From the time he began choosing his own books from the library, he chose science. Harry believes, without exception, that for everything existing, there is a natural reason. Harry is atheist, but more than that, he believes that when we're born, we're given only existence. Everything we do from there, what we learn and what we encounter, gives us value or not. Most of us have that choice and those who don't are the ones who need our help.

In Harry's world, the "room" of the title is a place of cosmic convergence, a repository of memory, and a place where pain and sadness resided and their memories linger. It's a place of both painful life and sad death that comes with regrets and desire for healing old wounds, or at least apologizing for old wrongs. The room is his mother's room, in a simple home in Orange County, New York. It's the place that Harry felt safest as a child, but as an adult it's where he's forced to relive uncomfortable memories.

Although Harry finally meets a woman who understands and truly loves him, the cosmos takes a different path. He's left to wonder if love can transcend a universe, and discovers that what goes wrong in life sometimes matters as much as what goes right.

This novel is intended as a work of imagination, but is not intended as a work of science fiction. In Harry's belief system, as in mine, science is not fiction. It is a reality of the most all-encompassing kind.

It concerns me at times about what kind of world we will leave our children. I worry about the growing influence of those who oppose new science. How they use their personal religious beliefs for their assertions, but then shun scrutiny. To talk about their religion is taboo. But religious groups that attempt to impose their beliefs on all of us, or influence government policies, are no longer off-limits. The very core of their beliefs is now open for debate.

My hope is that some day, those who believe in reason will be able to influence the course of history as much as those of faith.

Chapter 1

It was difficult to get out of bed today, but because it's Saturday, at least I wasn't awakened by the alarm. I lifted the edge of the window shade but let it down again when the bright light hurt my eyes. Sarah was dropping Kaela and Lainey off in a couple of hours and I still hadn't thought of something for us to do. I needed to tell them today that their grandmother is dying. I didn't want the news to weigh upon their whole visit, so I decided I'd tell them later in the day. I wasn't sure how Kaela would take it but Lainey understood death in such a basic way that I assumed she'd be alright.

It was over a year since Sarah and I split up and the divorce was finalized just a few weeks ago. It stung again when it was final, but with Mom dying, it was a one-two punch. Although Kaela was only 8 and Lainey 6, for at least those years the girls were able to fill a void for Mom after my brother Malcolm left. The sicker Mom got, the more pissed I was at my younger brother. He could never justify becoming angry at Mom and me. Just before he left for good, he began to perseverate on things. When our father was out, Malcolm began to repeatedly point out how Mom named me Harry after her Dad, while he was named after our father's father. He complained that he always got the short end of the stick.

When we were little, Malcolm was so often afraid. But he always stuck with me when our father was abusive. We began to sense when that bastard was close to becoming physical, so we slipped upstairs to Mom's room. Her deep closet was the best place to hide until everything blew over.

Our father moved out of Mom's room long before we could remember, choosing to sleep in the small room downstairs. He had his couch, his TV, and kept all his hunting and fishing gear in there. It was such a relief when he stayed in there all day. My brother and I never went into that room, but passing by when the door was open, we could see a huge pile of hunting magazines on the floor by the door. They always looked untouched, not a crinkle. I wondered why he bothered to keep getting them when it was obvious that he never read them.

Harry Ladd was finally able to get away from his father and make it upstairs. His father, Henry, was such an imposing presence when he was home. Everything had to revolve around him. When he was outside his room, he would walk around loudly, making sure that his presence was known. Even if Harry and Malcolm were talking, when Henry spoke, they stopped. No one in the house had anything more important to say.

Henry wasn't a tall man, thin build, but now with a larger waist and bottom compiled from years of sitting in his eighteen wheeler, as he transported goods around the county. He would shave, but only after the scruffiness was far too obvious and even then he would miss patches.

He had been on edge all day and Harry knew it was just a matter of time before there was trouble.

It wasn't even three o'clock and Henry insisted on having his dinner early. All it took was to have them all together at the table. His mother, Rue, was hurt but Harry couldn't stay around. He was afraid his father would remember why he got angry in the first place. But for the moment, his father was distracted. Henry was yelling at Rue about why it was her own fault that he pushed her down.

Harry was worried that his brother, Malcolm, might still be down-stairs. But when he opened the door to his mother's closet, he saw Malcolm inside. He found him frightened and sitting in the back cor-ner with the small battery lantern they always left in there. Harry crawled inside, closing the door, and sat against the wall. Malcolm was only ten years old and Harry looked out for his little brother as best he could. After all, Harry had two more years of experience with their father. But Harry could only do so much.

They felt safe for now. Their father would never find them in their mother's closet. They knew he never bothered to put in any effort once they hid. They could wait it out in there. The wooden floor even had a small gap between the boards where they heard sounds that carried up from the hall below. It was hard to make out words, but they could hear the intensity of the conversation.

"My stomach hurts," Harry said. "I didn't mean to waste my supper."

Malcolm, still shivering from time to time, just looked at Harry.

"I wasn't talking back," Harry continued. "I was just trying to tell him that I didn't feel well. He pushed Mom down. She tried to stop him when he slapped me, and he just pushed her out of the way. He got me only once when he saw that he hurt her."

Malcolm finally spoke.

"You have a red mark on your face."

"He got me good with that one shot," Harry said.

Harry put his hand to his face and flinched as he touched the spot where he was slapped.

"Why is he always mad, Harry?"

"I don't know, Malcolm. I wish I knew."

In a quiet moment they heard the smash of something being thrown against the wall downstairs.

Their father, Henry, was tired of blaming his wife, Rue, for what he had done so he threw his glass against the wall and stormed off to his room. It struck the framed photograph of Rue's parents and cracked the glass from bottom left to top right. Earlier, she struck her leg on the table when he pushed her down. But the pain in her heart hurt worse when he split the glass covering that photograph. She would later move it to the wall in her room, but would never get the glass replaced.

After the sound, Harry and Malcolm heard it go silent downstairs, so a short time later, Harry cracked open the door and peeked through the slit into the room. There on the wall he saw the photograph of Mom's parents. It was surrounded by light. He knew that it normally hung downstairs, but now it was here with a crack in the glass. They waited inside for a while, but once convinced their father had gone away, the boys came out and sat on their mother's bed. Harry looked toward the door and found it strange that the picture was gone, as was the light. They had only waited inside the closet for a few more minutes, Harry thought, there was barely enough time for Mom to remove it. Besides, they would have heard her on the stairs.

Rue struggled to clean up the mess in the kitchen, favoring her injured leg, but making it increasingly worse. She couldn't help herself. If Henry were to continue to walk past the mess, she knew he would take out his displeasure on the boys. When Rue finished, she took a small hammer from the drawer, removed the photograph from the wall, and pulled out the hanger.

The boys could hear their mother struggling to walk up the stairs. When she got to her bedroom, Harry saw her holding the photograph he saw hanging just minutes ago. Harry was puzzled as he watched his Mom hang it in the same spot. Rue finished hanging the photograph and put the hammer on her night table, then collapsed onto her bed. With the additional damage she had done, the pain had gotten so great that she was unable to get out of bed for days.

"Harry, please go next door and ask Ruth to come by. Please tell her that I need her help," Rue said. "You don't have to worry about your father. He's in his room."

Henry knew he'd gone too far, so he decided he would make himself scarce for a few days, sleeping in the back room of the trucking office where he worked. His regret didn't come from conscience. It was from a selfish fear he would cross a line, and lose the woman who waited on him hand and foot.

I had finally been able to keep the bad parts of my past out of mind, but ever since Mom took a turn for the worse, I couldn't help myself from dwelling on it. I put on a pot of coffee and looked into the refrigerator to see if there was creamer. I could smell stale coffee grounds permeating the area near the counter. It wasn't like me to forget the trash until it was ripe, but I had so much on my mind. I meant to pick up groceries to make something for my daughters to eat, but sandwiches from the deli next door would have to do for supper later.

As the coffee brewed, I went to wash and get dressed, not paying much attention to what I wore. Although this apartment was supposed to be temporary, I hadn't done well enough to move. I planned on renting a larger one when I could, so having the children stay overnight would be appealing to them. Perhaps the only redeeming qualities this place had were the people around here and my view of the town center. I really enjoyed sitting at the window and watching the people.

Although my apartment was small, I loved living in this little section of town. The stores in a row were small businesses, some with apartments above, but they all had the look of old style homes and shops. Next to the tavern are a small gift shop, print shop, pizzeria and antique store. On the opposite side there's the car parts store, the deli, a bar in the basement below the parts store and the deli, and the computer repair shop under my apartment. In addition to the charmed feel of this small town center, there was the warmth of the people who inhabited the area's apartments, houses and businesses.

Sarah and I sold our home, which had far more room for storage, so I had to find places for all the possessions I'd accumulated. One was a large telescope I carried down and up and down again, to the small paved area in the back. The lot behind the stores is shielded from some of the street lamps, but the ambient light is still a bit strong to look at anything more than the moon and planets. When we were a family at home, I would ask the girls to look through the scope with me. Once, after several nights of calling them out to look at Jupiter and Saturn, they asked why I kept looking at the same planets. I explained about the movement of Jupiter's moons and how in awe I was looking at another world with my own eyes. I told them that it was all beautiful, but never as beautiful as them.

The night sky gave focus to so much vastness that it gave me a true sense of how really tiny we are. One tiny person on a small blue dot circling an insignificant sun at the far edge of our galaxy, filled with billions of suns and a universe filled with billions of other galaxies. I find it hard to understand why anyone would think the cosmos cared about any one of us.

I enjoy talking with the girls about all of these things. No matter how young they are or how much they grasp, I always tell them what I consider to be the truth. I'm often surprised at how much they are able to understand and I want them to grow up with knowledge in science. My hope is for it to become so natural that they'd continue to have an interest and want to know more. Science has always been so important to me and is the first subject I look for when the girls bring their report cards to show me. Carl Sagan, my favorite scientist and writer, once said that we live in a society exquisitely dependent on science and technology, in which hardly anyone knows anything about science and technology. I wasn't going to let my girls end up like those people.

Sarah was picking up the girls at 9 PM as she does every other Saturday when they visited. She was prompt when getting them but the time she dropped them off would vary. Before the girls went home, I often explained to them how I would soon be doing well enough to find a place where they could have their own room. I could see in their eyes that they didn't believe I could, but they didn't want to dash my hope.

Sarah moved back with her parents in Westchester, who were only happy to give her and the children the lower level of their home and all the help they need. I'm happy that the children have good schools, nice things and a comfortable home. I pay what I can for the girls and to Sarah, but her parents have much more to offer. Her parents are well off and when Sarah and I were together, they never hesitated to point that out. It was obvious they never thought I was good enough for her.

Her father especially dislikes me. Being a man of faith, he has no patience for my views. He insists that raising the girls without God is nothing short of abuse, but ignores that Sarah feels the same way I do. He attributes that to exposure to me.

As much as both her parents disliked me, I could only feel grateful that they were there to take care of the girls, even if they used it to show how little I had left to give. I can't accept that a person's monetary worth makes them who they are. Maybe I have an idealistic view, since I hadn't done as well as hoped, but knew I could do better. I would do better.

Sarah was doing well now. She finished the last few courses needed to complete her degree and took a job at a bank where she planned to work herself up to manager. She was always good with money, so thorough. I knew she would do alright without me. I heard from the girls that there was a man who came around recently and their Mom and he would go out for the evening. I told the girls that it was OK because their mother needs to have a friend to talk to, but you could see that it made them a little sad. I imagined why it would be hard for them. They loved both of us and innately felt the finality when they saw their mom with someone other than me. I tried to show them I wasn't hurt and that I was happy for their mom. But it did hurt, if even a little.

Lainey often asked me to come to Westchester so I could see her room. She was proud of the drawings she wanted to show me and didn't understand why I wouldn't go. She's just a little girl, learning about new things and I had to miss waking up with her on my shoulder, seeing her come home from school and watching her explore all the new things in her life. Kaela is my big girl, 8 years old and wise beyond her years. They are two sides of a coin, Lainey slowly developing a creative edge while Kaela is organized and practical. Whenever they visited, I was reminded of how much I missed being a family, but what could I do? Sarah believed that she did what was best for her and the kids and maybe she was right. It couldn't be good for them to grow up in a house where their parents had no real love for each other.

Before they were born, Sarah was my friend through all the rough times. I wasn't exactly sure when, but after we had the children we drifted apart. When she left, Sarah insisted that her energies would be better spent on just the girls. Although I had often been cold and sometimes angry, there were things about Sarah that I had to deal with as well. She instructed me at times about what or what not to say to the girls. It was continually pointed out that other friends of hers were doing better and had bigger houses. Anytime I made any progress or received a pay raise, it was never enough.

The people we were when we first met were gone. She became cold and I knew it could only go on for so long. I questioned, but never resisted her leaving because inside I felt that she was most likely right. We stopped giving each other what we needed, and I felt sorry that the girls had to be affected by it all. Sarah knew I thought of her as a good mother; when it came to the girls she always put them first. After we separated, our conversations, although minimal, were nonetheless civil, just as long as we kept them to logistics. Still, as much as I wanted more details about the things the girls did, it was best that I just get that from them.

I had been daydreaming so long that it surprised me a bit when I heard the tap on a horn. When I looked out the window, Sarah saw me so she shuffled the girls out of the car and they ran up the creaky stairs to my apartment. I loved the sound of their multiple little steps as they came up. The girls had their small backpacks that I knew would be properly packed with lunch, healthy snacks, pencils, paper and other personal items. Sarah was meticulous about those things. She expected I would have forgotten to pick up some fruits and snacks for them.

When they reached the top of the stairs, I saw my girls with neatly tied-back hair and nice clean clothes. They had on the same style shirts, but Kaela had on light blue and Lainey wore red. Their jackets matched and both wore jeans and little brown boots. With the money I contributed, Sarah's salary and her parents providing the home, Sarah could finally give the girls the things she considered important.

"Mom said she'll be back at nine to get us," Kaela said, although it was the same each visit.

Lainey looked a little sad and I asked her why.

"I missed you Dad. My picture was up in the art show at school and Mom went."

I bent down and looked at her.

"You know that I love you two and I would have been there if I could."

Somehow it was enough for now and I watched her face change to a small smile as she pulled a wrinkled piece of paper from her backpack.

"I brought it so you can see." She said smiling ear to ear.

It was a pencil drawing of a little girl and a man holding hands.

"It's you and me, Dad."

"It's beautiful, Lainey," I said as I turned and held it up toward the window.

I didn't want her to see in my face that I felt sad she couldn't see me all the time. From the day they were born, I maybe worried too much about the girls. When they were sick I always wished I could take it away, be sick for them. Maybe I was often too worried, but I couldn't help myself. I wanted to protect them from everything, even though I knew deep inside that I couldn't.

I could tell that Kaela also missed me but being the responsible one she already made herself comfortable on the couch and was doing left-over homework. She pulled out extra school papers with red circled marks at the top, carefully spreading them so I would see. She wanted me to look at them, but was waiting for me to notice on my own. Kaela beamed as I picked up the papers.

"You are doing so well, Kaela."

"Dad, I got all hundreds in math this semester," she said. "My teacher said I was the only one."

I sat down for a moment and looked over all the rest of her papers, acknowledging how well she did in all the subjects. I was so very happy with the way Kaela was growing up, how they both were. Since Sarah and I split, Kaela became more protective of her little sister. She held Lainey's hand to cross the street, made sure she closed her jacket, and other things she saw her mom do. The girls were taking our divorce well and I was comforted by that. What I wanted the most was for them to be happy. I could deal with anything else if I knew they were.

I had put little thought into what we could do today as I was happy just to see them, but I knew that they were expecting some activity. I asked them if they wanted to hike in Black Rock Forest, knowing they loved it there.

"That would be great, Dad," Kaela said, already beginning to stand.

Lainey agreed as well, so we packed up their lunches and a few of their snacks and started down the stairs to the car.

In late spring, the Hudson Valley had to be one of the most beautiful places on the planet. Hiking in Black Rock was awesome by itself, but we turned it into a science expedition by looking for little fossils in the rocks. The new leaves were so pure and the streams were full from melt off, making the waterfalls compelling. We sat on a large rock just talking as we watched the water crash white as it hit the rocks at the bottom. Something about the sound was soothing, peaceful. I got up to throw a few stones into the water while the girls continued to sit on the large rock and talk. I didn't know what the future had in store for them, but I could see that they would tackle it together. Malcolm and I had stopped talking. I knew that would never happen to them. They'll always have each other.

When we moved on, we came to the top of the hill where there was a small lake, so still and clear. Kaela reached in and cupped a salamander in her hands.

"You know, Kaela, it was your cousin three hundred and forty million years ago."

"Oh, Dad," said Lainey.

"No really, give or take a few million or so."

I saw at first they were puzzled, but when Kaela gently placed the sala-mander back in the lake. I saw that she was starting to understand. I explained that we humans were the only animal on earth that spends so much time and energy denying what we really are.

"We now know that we're related to every bit of life on the planet," I told them. "That's why it's important that we treat everything with respect. If you would like, some time I will tell you why even life itself owes its existence to long dead stars."

Kaela said she would like that, while Lainey had gone back to picking up round stones to toss into the water.

We continued our conversation as we walked along the narrow road back to the car. I told them how their grandmother would bring Malcolm and me to these spots when we were little and how much fun we had hiking. Mom had gotten too old to hike the trails with us, but at least I continued the tradition. Although there were playgrounds in the county, there wasn't a playground anywhere that compared to Black Rock.

"Are we going to visit Grandma today?" Kaela asked.

"Not today, sweetheart. She's not feeling well."

"Maybe we can cheer her up," Lainey added.

"I'm sure of that," I said. "But she needs to rest today".

I would tell them soon enough, but it wasn't the best time.

When we got to the stream that flowed along the top of the road, we side-tracked to walk on the rocks in the middle. The girls laughed when I lost my footing and plopped into the stream. It wasn't deep but my socks and shoes were soaked.

"Sure, go ahead and laugh," I said. "I meant to do that."

They laughed again.

"You're going to squish when you walk Daddy," Lainey said.

"Daddy wants to squish when he walks," Kaela added, and winked at me.

The road was a shortcut back to the lot but was worth taking because it had a distant view of the railroad trestle and the Moodna Valley at the north end of Schunemunk Mountain. The valley had turned a beautiful green and you could see the patterns made by tractors on the newly-seeded farms below. We could see a smattering of farm houses and the town beyond. With all the roads obscured by the trees, the farms were islands in a sea of green stretching far beyond what we could see.

On the opposite side of the road, there was a towering rock formation. I imagined that although created ages ago, it had barely changed in thousands of years. The dirt on each side was worn away from heavy rains that pour down from the mountain above. Some of the streams only appeared with spring melt off and the rains but you could see the channels they left behind. They were often the best places to find fossils since they exposed the rocks in their path.

A short while later we reached the car and Lainey took a map from the pamphlet bin at the start of the trail. She did every time we came and made a small pile of them on the shelf in my apartment. Every so often, I would gather them up and bring them back with us so they wouldn't go to waste.

We took a moment to clean off the mud caking our boots before getting in. I kept a small brush in the trunk but I never worried too much about getting dirt in the car. It was old and I had given up on keeping it clean. As I left the lot, I could tell they had fun when they both turned back to stare as we drove away.

In the car, I saw Kaela looked a little puzzled, so I asked her why.

"Why doesn't Uncle Malcolm come to visit and why don't we get to meet Brian?" she asked.

"I wish I knew, sweetheart. There is a lot about your Uncle Malcolm I don't understand."

"Can we call Brian?" Lainey asked.

"I'm not sure that's such a good idea and I don't have the number anyway," I told them.

"Well, Kaela and I are always going to stay together," Lainey said.

"I'm counting on it," I told them. "I know you will."

When we got back, we stopped at the deli next door to pick up some sandwiches and salads for dinner. The deli had been there for years, owned by Ben Cahill who took it over when his father passed away. Ben was the quintessential deli man with a large chest, full white butcher's apron and a neatly cropped silver mustache.

The shop had wooden floors which he always kept clean. He left it old style, with hanging cheeses and the traditional long white refrigerated counter where he stored the daily offerings of cold cuts and other meats. There was the large walk-in refrigerator in the back with a big silver door and long chrome handle. To the side, he had a handful of small tables where his customers could sit and eat. As I approached the counter, the smell of the cheeses permeated my nose and made me hungry. Ben rang up the charge for a woman buying some meats and then saw us.

"Harry, you have such beautiful girls."

"Thanks Ben. They're growing so fast."

"Hi, Mr. Cahill," Kaela and Lainey said.

"Would you like the usual?" Ben asked the girls.

When they nodded, he began to prepare the food and they went over to one of the tables to sit and wait. It was funny how Lainey always looked to Kaela for guidance with everything, even down to the food they both ordered. It would be two ham and American cheese sandwiches on plain rolls with just a little mayonnaise. They even both enjoyed the small tub of cole slaw Ben would give on the side. Orange juice for both to top it off. It made me happy they preferred that to soda.

"I'll take a hero, Ben, Swiss cheese with all the veggies you have and a little mayo."

"You got it, Harry. How is your mother doing?"

"As well as can be expected," I told him.

Ben knew that Mom had been diagnosed with brain cancer and was not expected to live much longer, and he seemed concerned about how I was taking it. I told him that I was comforted by the fact she could stay at home and was provided nursing care so she wouldn't have to spend her last days in a hospital. The doctors told me that all she had was a few days more, at most. I explained that I didn't want the girls to see their grandmother as sick as she was, so I had planned to go and stay with Mom tomorrow.

I took the week as vacation so I could spend some time with her before she passed, but I needed today to tell the girls. The nurse was going to call me if Mom's condition worsened. Ben was a good listener and he had dutifully taken on the job of town sounding board. He was the one who kept the neighborhood informed of anything any of us was going through.

When Ben finished getting our food he placed the bag on the counter.

"Here you go, Harry. It's a shame about your mother."

"Thanks, Ben."

I handed him the money with an extra ten dollars.

"That's the last ten I owe you for the food tab. I appreciate it," I told him.

The girls saw that Ben was finished, so they came up to the counter.

"Thanks, Mr. Cahill," the girls said.

We took our bag and left.

In the apartment, I removed a few items from the coffee table and put out mats so we could eat there. For the moment the girls seemed happy, as if we were a family in our home. We talked more about their school and I asked how their piano lessons were coming along. They were both more excited to talk about how their Grandpa Hanson bought them a new computer and gave each of them money to buy a game they wanted. I thought it must be nice to be able to give the girls not only what they needed but also some extra things they wanted. When we were together in our home, they seemed to be satisfied with what they had. Even though I couldn't afford everything, they had my love. That was always enough for them.

"So are you happy?" I asked.

Lainey nodded and Kaela said, "Yeah, ah yes, Dad, we are."

"That's all I ever want for you two. I'm glad to hear it."

I realized that once the girls grew into their own lives, I would be more alone. I would have had Malcolm, but he had been gone for so many years. As I did, he hated our father but never forgave our mother for her inaction when he physically and verbally abused us. I never blamed Mom since she was a victim herself, but Malcolm did. It was hard for all of us to deal with, but had bitten him more.

I couldn't even imagine beating my children as my father beat us. At first I wondered what I did wrong, why I deserved to be beaten. As I got older, I realized that I hadn't done anything out of the ordinary, nothing wrong. Up to the day he died, I never was able to figure out what twisted reasoning he used to justify his actions to himself.

Malcolm, being younger, always seemed stunned by the actions of our father. I tried to intervene in the beginning, but when I did I only made things worse. Mom learned earlier not to interfere because it also led to more trouble for all of us. I was able to ignore the yelling. It was the beatings with the belt that angered me most. Malcolm couldn't blow off any of it and was always frightened. I understood who to blame from the beginning, but Malcolm never did.

Since our father died six years ago, Mom began to regret that she stayed with him, that she lost Malcolm. I got a message to him when our father died but he never attended the funeral. I would have skipped it also if not for Mom. She needed me there. I only knew how Malcolm was through a couple of his old friends because he stopped calling me years ago. He realized I could never be angry at Mom for not removing us from the abuse.

Malcolm moved to New Jersey when he finished school, got a decent job in business and married a woman name Julia. They had a son, Brian, and I heard that they were happy. I imagined he lived in a tidy little house with a practical car on a tree-lined street in suburbia. Julia would be driving a minivan, shuffling Brian off to soccer. I pictured that their lawn would be properly tended to and inside the two-car garage, on the wall would be all the hanging tools Malcolm used to keep his yard nice.

I hadn't noticed the time until there was barely a half hour left before Sarah was picking the girls up and I needed to tell them about their grandmother. They already knew that she was sick, but they didn't real-ize how sick she was. I started by telling them how their grandmother was so happy watching them grow into wonderful young ladies.

"Girls, your grandmother won't be with us much longer," I told them.

"But Dad, where is Grandma Ladd going?" Lainey asked.

"She is dying, Lainey."

"My teacher told me that when people die they go to heaven," said Kaela. "Mom says she is not sure."

"Well, your mom is right. Nobody really knows. Nobody is really sure."

I explained that they should never believe someone who tells them that we live forever just because they say so. I needed extraordinary evidence for such amazing claims and never saw anything to convince me so far. There are some who believe that there are people with wings like a bird, a snake that talked and also relish in telling their children a story in which every species of animal on earth owed its existence to a man who built a large boat. To me, it was obvious that these stories were never meant to be taken literally.

"Wishing something were so, doesn't make it so," I told them.

I never believed in God, but when the girls were born, I stopped being silent. I was abhorred by the religious groups who professed to know all the answers and continually blamed those with my views for the ills of the planet. If they insisted on engaging in politics and influencing decisions that affect my children's future, then there would be no hands off. The very core of their reasoning must be open to debate. Even so young, my girls knew that they would never hear any stories of myth from me. Even if religion could provide some small comfort at times, I always believed it did more harm than good.

"What I do know is that it would be a shame to waste precious moments counting on another life while missing the beautiful one you already have," I told them.

I let them know how much their grandmother loved them and about how thrilled she was when they were born. We talked about some of the good times we all had. Mom always made sure to bring the candies the girls liked when she came to see them in our home. She loved it even more when she had them for the day at her house. The way the girls described those days sounded as though they were full of thoughtful activities. Having had two boys, the girls were a whole new experience for her.

The girls never knew my father. He died just a month before Lainey was born and Kaela was too young then to remember him. I was relieved about that. Sarah and I would never have let the girls go to Mom's house if my father was alive. Mom was crushed when Sarah left with the girls and she got to see them much less often. But I did my best to bring them by. At least they had their grandmother for the time that they did.

"She really loves you two so much," I said.

Sarah pulled up and tapped the horn, so I helped pack up their things and gave them a hug.

"Girls, I love you both. I will send your love to Grandma Ladd. I am sorry you couldn't visit with her today, but I didn't want you to see her this ill. I'll call you from there tomorrow, so you can talk with her."

"I had a good time today. Thanks Dad," Kaela said.

I walked them to the stairs and hugged them once more, lifting them up, and giving them a kiss. As they walked down to their mom, Lainey stopped on the stairs and turned to look at me.

"I'm sorry that Grandma is dying, Dad."

"Me too, Lainey," I said. "We will miss her."

From the window, I watched them talking to Sarah as they were getting into the car. I couldn't hear what they were saying but I guessed it would be about their Grandma Ladd. I saw Sarah get out and come around to take their shoes. She noticed they were still dirty from the hike and tapped them together to shake off the dirt before placing them in the trunk. As they pulled away from the curb, I saw Lainey turn and look up. When she saw me she waved goodbye and kept looking as Sarah drove away.

Chapter 2

With the evening so mild, I put on my Ingrid Michaelson CD and listened as I sat by the open window to watch the people walk by. I enjoy putting a soundtrack to real life; it makes the goings on below all that more interesting. I could hear people talking as they walked past, and looking down the block I saw a group of people entering Brooks Tavern.

Brice Brooks had set up his outside tables for the first time this spring and his daughter Lacie was taking an order at one. The tavern is an old style place inside, with a long bar and a half dozen booths located in the back. It has the original plank wood floor, comfortably worn, but always kept clean.

Brice moved to the U.S. from England twenty years ago and had been running the tavern ever since. Lacie was a counselor on the weekdays, but she enjoyed working at the tavern on Friday and Saturday nights. It gave her a little extra money and she loved being around her dad. She was just nine when her dad brought them here. Brice still had a pronounced British accent, but his daughter had just a hint.

There were only the two of them since her mom passed away when Lacie was seven. Brice and his wife saved for years in order to move to the states and open a small business. After she died, he wanted to do what she always dreamed for them and their daughter. Brice saved for two more years, sold their home and then moved to America.

I called the evening nurse at Mom's house and she told me how Mom was sitting up today but she was increasingly becoming delusional. Nurse Barnes said Mom thought that her sons were out playing, and would be getting home soon. She asked her to check on them. She also told me that Mom looked anxious when she spoke about her husband. She continually called Ms. Barnes "Ruth." I explained that my mother's neighbor and friend, Ruth Lambert, was likely who she believed her to be.

"She died decades ago. At least it's good that she sees you as someone who comforted her," I said.

"Your mother has been back in bed since seven o'clock and she's sleeping well," she told me.

I knew that her mind might be affected because the doctor told me that it might, but it was upsetting now that it was happening.

"Thank you for taking such great care of my mother."

"You're welcome, Mr. Ladd. I will be here until eight in the morning if you wish to call. Otherwise, Grace takes over and will be expecting you."

"Thanks."

Since Mom was diagnosed as terminal, she had taken it well. I was proud of how she faced her illness with courage. We both decided to keep the seriousness of it from the girls until now because we believed it was best. We had no reason to tell them until it was necessary. Today it was.

With the delusions Ms Barnes told me about, I could understand why Mom saw her as Ruth. She was the only friend Mom turned to when she needed to talk. I wondered what was worse, to realize she was dying, or in her mind to live in the past. I hoped that when she saw me grown it wouldn't frighten her and it troubled me that she believed my father was alive. I hoped I could somehow comfort her.

My thoughts were so busy it was hard to stop them from racing through my head. I felt a few beers might dull them for a while. I grabbed my wallet, cell phone and keys and headed for Brooks.

As I was walked toward the tavern, I saw Lacie serving food at a table outside. She looked at me and smiled, then turned back to what she was doing. Lacie is seven years younger than me, adorable, small-framed and soft-spoken. Her light brown hair falls well below her shoulders, parted in front, hiding the tops of her large deep green eyes. We talked a few times and I really enjoyed her company.

As I got closer, I heard the low sound of music. They kept it quiet outside so it wouldn't disturb the people who live nearby. It was classical music that always played outside and in the back near the booths.

Brice was partial to romantic pieces, Chopin, Debussy. He believed it added the right touch. The bar area was reserved for the television, which Brice switched between sports games and CNN.

As I walked in, I nodded hello to a few of the regulars, and sat down at an empty stool near the far end of the bar. The stools closest to the TV always filled first. The regulars were of course debating about the baseball game. They all enjoyed the little squabbles, even though Pete always thought he'd prevailed on most of the points. The wall behind the bar had a shelf high up, running the whole length and filled with an array of old bottles. There were so many shapes, colors and shades of glass. I imagine Brice knew where each bottle came from.

There were some young couples sitting in the booths in the back. They come to Brook's from time to time because, even with the music, it was still a quiet enough place to talk. For the regulars, it was a clean well-lit place. For some of them, it was the only place they could go to keep from being alone. Brice never allowed any trouble and people respected that. There was a dart board near the front window where a young man in his twenties was daring his friends to play a rematch with him. There were so many conversations that they were reduced to a low drone in the background.

Before I sat down, Lacie went into the back to place another order. When she came out, she looked around until she saw where I was sitting. She came over and put her hand on my leg.

"Hi, Harry. Are you going to be here awhile?"

I told her I wasn't sure. I didn't know how long I would stay.

"I really wish that you would stay. Maybe we could talk a little later," she said.

"I will then," I told her, and she went back to her customers.

Brice was pouring drinks at the bar. When he saw me, he motioned that he would be right over. He was a stocky guy, large-armed, and you could see experience in his face right up to the grey mix in his hair. With Lacie being small, I assumed she must have taken after her mom.

Brice never asked what I wanted. I was stopping in at least once a week lately and he made a point to remember. He poured a beer from the tap and brought it over. As always, the first one he poured into a frosted glass. Brice had a deep freezer box under the back counter where he stored dozens of glasses at a time for his customers who ordered tap.

"Here you go, Harry. How are you feeling tonight?"

With everything on my mind, I'm sure it showed on my face. I had talked with Brice the week before when Mom was not doing as badly.

"Thanks for asking. Actually, Mom is not doing so well."

Brice turned serious.

"Sorry to hear that Harry," he said, and he focused his attention on me.

He always had a sympathetic ear and it was clear that he meant the things he said.

"Thanks. We all lose someone we love," I said, forcing a small smile.

"Do you find comfort in prayer, Harry?"

"I've always been an atheist, Brice. I have no interest in religion."

"Well, to tell you the truth, Harry, I stopped believing since my wife passed away years ago. It was hard to hear the priest tell me that God had a plan, and it was not for us to know. I just couldn't tell that to Lacie. Lacie is everything to me and I felt I would be lying to her. There is so much of her mom in her."

"Your wife must have been beautiful," I told him, and thought of Lacie.

"She was," he said. "I always try to keep her alive in Lacie's heart. On Lacie's birthdays, one of my presents is always something that was her mother's. When I give it to her, she thinks of her mother and cries. She told me never to let that stop me, as long as there were still treasures."

"I wish that my father had been a tenth of the one you are," I told him.

"Thanks, Harry."

He seemed grateful that I made him think of his wife and that he was able to talk about her. It made him smile as he went back to serving drinks.

I was glad that I stopped in. I too needed a clean, well-lit place tonight, a place to not be alone. The beer was beginning to dull the uncomfortable thoughts and it was nice to see people enjoying life. It was hard for me when Sarah first left. Even now I feel a little guilty just looking at Lacie or any other woman, although there's no reason to feel that way.

I get feelings that I should be at home with my family, tucking my children into bed. After eleven years of marriage, those are hard thoughts to break, like changing sides of a bed. But even with the way things turned out, I was thrilled about my daughters, to have them in my life. So why should I complain? Everyone has serious problems at one time or another. No matter how bad things get, there's always somebody else who has it worse. Given time, we can get over anything.

I find it funny we believe every age to be the most significant time in history. Just as every generation believes they belong to the pinnacle of time. I can't understand why people don't see that everything we are, we create. Units of time, all that we build: whatever. We make it all up. We're restricted to the natural rhythm of the earth, but we interpret it as it pleases us to do so. From the simplest profession to the most elaborate, much of our societal perceived worth is created by us.

Sometimes I feel embarrassed to be human, because we consume the planet's resources without the slightest consideration for future generations, or choose to remain complacent to those who hoard those resources for profit. It disturbed me that at the very time we needed new innovations the most, America elected a man willing to let the energy companies write his first energy bill. We had become a government for the few people by the few people.

With all of our most brilliant achievements in technology, we continue to power it all with gook from the ground. I saw clips of President Kennedy from the 1960s who called upon the scientific community to take America to the moon and they rose to the challenge. He also encouraged citizens to ask what they could do for their country. Where is the leadership today? Who will challenge America to develop new energy technologies, especially now that the stakes are so high? America is ripe for new challenges, new sacrifices. But always the opportunity is squandered, all as we are led into a war, succeeding only to create continuous resources for those who are profiting from it.

The game ended, so Brice switched the television to news. I couldn't hear it from where I was, but when I saw the newscasters, I thought of how unemotional they are when they announce the death of a celebrity or other public figure. They don't care, no one really cares. Life goes on and that's just the way it is. Like a shallow look of sorrow when people view an accident scene. What most are really distraught about is that it reminds them of their own mortality. I find it fascinating and a little bizarre when I hear about preachers who say that an early demise or a confrontation with disaster was somehow brought upon the victims because they displeased their God.

Sometimes I feel so sorry for people. Other times their ignorance makes me mad as hell. Last week in Kansas, a tornado touched down and wiped out an entire neighborhood. When they interviewed a woman who lived in the only house spared by this killer, all she could say was that God had spared her. Didn't she see the destruction all around her? Were her friends and neighbors unworthy? Good people were killed all around her, yet she was convinced her God selected only her and her house to be saved. Those were the things that made me angry. How could the human race ever advance if so many people were convinced they had little control over their own lives?

But then there's the good in people. In a mine collapse a couple of years ago, an entire town came out to help dig, trying to save over a dozen men trapped below. They worked in dire conditions with little sleep for days. Those who could dig, dug, while those who couldn't, served the others food and water to keep them going. Their tireless efforts paid off and the miners were saved. Here was a shining example of the goodness of humanity only to be diminished by the news organizations whose headlines called it an act of God. All the efforts of those amazing people became incidental.

When were people going to wake up to the fact that it's only us who can make a difference? Some people employ such platitudes to hide their true existence. They bathe themselves in rituals offered by their religions in order to spare themselves from reality.

After filling the empty glasses along the bar, Brice walked over with the local newspaper.

"Have you seen the paper today, Harry?"

"Thanks, I would like to look at it," I told him.

He handed me The Times Herald Record, a local paper. Most times, I only cared to read the column from Beth Quinn on Mondays. Most of her columns were a welcome rant against the President and the war. I need to hear someone tell it like it is. I looked at the events that were going on in the area tomorrow, knowing full well I would be with Mom. I smiled as I passed the astrology column, picturing groups of readers aligning their day to the ramblings of a phony. How sad I thought it was, to believe that somehow vague sentences spoke of them person-ally. Why actually live when you can open the paper and find out what you should be doing that day. The most telling part of it all is that almost every newspaper in the country has an astrology column while only a small handful have, at best, a weekly column about science.

Flipping further through the pages, I stopped to read the obituaries, something I hadn't done before. I read the kind words from loved ones about the family member they lost. What would I say about Mom? She never worked outside the home, no special activities and she had no friends to speak of. My father kept her timid for so many years that she backed away from any friends she had, years ago. The only person she did talk with was her neighbor, Ruth, who died decades ago.

I remember how hard it was for Mom to find something to write when my father died. She sat staring at a blank page, tapping the pencil and although she tried not to, she couldn't help but cry. Mom felt embarrassed when I saw her cry. There was a conflict in her between a sense of relief and her lost sense of purpose. When she finally finished, his obituary contained only a list of the schools he attended, where he worked and those he left behind.

Malcolm moved from the area years before that, and when I reached him to tell him our father died, he never even asked about Mom, and never came. That was the part that hurt her the most. She had truly lost Malcolm. That was the last time I spoke with him. I selfishly thought for a moment that maybe if I too had made a clean break with the past, I could have kept my family together. I might be as happy as Malcolm's friend Jeff told me Malcolm was. I just could never abandon Mom like Malcolm did. Mom never meant to hurt us.

The one thing I could write about Mom was how she is loved by her son and two granddaughters. I had every intention of listing Malcolm. He wouldn't know anyway. He wouldn't care if he did find out. She raised him, and the least he should do is not complain if I gave Mom the dignity of having him listed.

After a few beers, I wanted something to eat so I grabbed my glass and went over to sit in one of the empty booths in back. There were only a couple of booths filled and I didn't want to eat at the bar. The booths had soft black seats, old and comfortably worn, with solid wooden tables. In the center of each table near the wall are small speakers for soft music. Next to it is ketchup, salt and pepper and on the other side a small ceramic tray of sugar and sweeteners. Everything is always clean. An American touch to old English charm presented in an authentic way. It's a comfortable place.

Lacie came out of the kitchen and I saw her notice that the stool I had been sitting on was empty. She looked disappointed for a moment that maybe I had gone after all, but when she looked toward the booths she saw me. She smiled and came over.

"I was thinking of having something to eat," I told her.

"I'll bring you a menu," she said.

"Thanks, Lacie, I won't need a menu. I would like the roasted boneless chicken," I said.

"I will go back and ask him to make it fresh for you," she told me. "It won't take too long, Harry. Can I bring you another beer?"

Normally, I would have had enough with a few, but I said yes. She went into the back to give my order to the cook and then brought the beer for me.

"Do you mind if I sit with you and talk?" she asked, but was already starting to sit down.

"Not at all, I would like that."

Lacie's voice was as soothing as she was and I really enjoyed talking with her. She just looked at me for a moment, not saying anything. I wondered what she was thinking about and I felt I had to say something.

"I really like your Dad, Lacie. You are fortunate to have him."

"Well you know, he told me that out of anyone that I talk to he likes you the best," she said, and deeply smiled.

I told her that I wish I had grown up with a father like him and that it was obvious she was the most important thing in his life.

"Speaking of the important things in life, I saw you earlier this evening with your girls," she said. "They're beautiful, you know."

"I love them more than life itself," I told her.

"So why did you split with your wife anyway?" she asked, leaning forward, elbows on the table.

I explained that at first I felt as if Sarah was my best friend, that I thought she did love me once. I told her how, after the girls were born, Sarah and I began to go in different directions. I was angry that we were drifting apart and as I got angrier, it drove her further away. I just made things worse but she was happy to let things get out of hand. It finally brought us to the point when she left.

"Soon after she left, I realized I wasn't angry anymore."

"Maybe, even though she left you, it was something you really wanted," Lacie added.

"I'm just not sure," I told her. "Maybe it was my fault, maybe it was hers. I just don't know anymore."

"What about you, Lacie? Is there someone you're seeing?"

"Well, not now. To tell you the truth, it's hard to find someone who interests me. I hope that doesn't sound too vain," she said.

"No. I kind of know what you mean. You want someone who you can really talk with," I told her.

"It can't be too much to ask, that I look for someone who makes me feel excited," Lacie said. "I need to be with someone who wants to explore things. I would rather be alone than be stuck in a relationship that isn't right."

"You're a gem, Lacie," I said. "From the times we've talked, I can see that. Don't ever think of settling."

"You're sweet Harry, Thanks."

Lacie went to get my food and, when she brought it back, she asked me if we could talk some more when she finished work at midnight. I told her that would be great and she went to care for her customers. This time, as she walked around the tavern, I found myself staring at her. I couldn't help looking at Lacie just a little bit differently than I had. I thought I saw a difference when she looked at me as well. My hands were beginning to sweat as I was thinking how great it would be to hold her.

Since Sarah left, I really never looked around to date. I just never cared. I was afraid that anyone I ever met would just do to me what Sarah did. With Lacie, it was somehow different. The way she looked at things masked the past's sour taste. I could actually see myself caring for someone in that way again. Lacie could be that person, I thought.

The tavern was beginning to wind down and the kitchen closed. I had finished my chicken and hadn't seen Lacie come in from the back yet. I got up to put my dishes in the plastic bin and then saw Lacie getting a couple beers from her Dad. As she walked over, I saw that she changed into a soft blue skirt and thin white cotton top. The shirt flowed beautifully around her breasts. I was wondering if she caught me looking at her or knew how great I thought she looked.

"I hope you feel like having one more with me," she said.

"I do feel like it," I told her.

She mentioned that her dad let her know about my mom and said how sorry she was to hear it. I thanked her for saying so.

"I have only a few memories of my mom," Lacie told me. "In one she was cutting and placing flowers in a vase that she put in the center of our large kitchen table. I watched her snip off little pieces repeatedly until they were just the right size for the way she wanted them arranged. With every snip I could smell them more. My dad told me years later that she always picked the flowers from her garden. It was in the rear of our house near the hill," she said. "I remember that from the back porch, it looked as if the flowers went into the sky. I may not have many memories of her, but the ones I have are special."

I loved the way Lacie grabbed my hand as she spoke, squeezing when she wanted to accent something. The more I looked at her, the more I wanted to stay. We talked for some time, telling each other little things about our lives. Lacie has a firm grip on reality. She knows what I believe in and what I don't, and she is fine with it. As with conversations in the past, I can see she thinks about some of the same things.

I'm in awe about how so many people are haunted by belief in the supernatural. It's difficult for me to understand what keeps them from questioning those who tell them extraordinary tales and why they would let others guide their lives. With so few people who understood these things, it was great to be able to speak about them without offending someone. I felt so comfortable talking with Lacie. She was what I needed right now and I was starting to hope we could be together but just not yet. As much as I wanted to, though, I had to think about Mom right now.

We were finishing our beer and it was half past midnight. I told Lacie how I was going to be with Mom the next morning and that I really should be going. I took a chance and asked her if we could go out some time when my life calmed down. She said she'd like that, which in itself made it so I wanted to stay, but I got up to put our glasses on the bar and pay my bill. I said goodbye to Lacie and gave a wave down the bar.

"Good night, Brice."

"Good night, Harry," he said. "I hope things go as well for you as they can."

What an insightful comment, I thought.

"Good night Harry," a couple of the regulars said.

"Good night folks. Have a nice Sunday."

"Harry, wait up. I'm just leaving. I'll walk out with you," Lacie said.

"Sure, I told her. I'll wait."

I stood for a moment while Lacie talked with her dad. She only worked here on Friday and Saturday nights and I heard her tell him that she loved him and would see him next Friday. He smiled and closed his eyes as she kissed him on the cheek. She picked up her thin jacket and we walked outside.

Chapter 3

We were standing outside the tavern and Lacie slipped on her jacket since there was a slight chill at this hour. The moon was bright over the library clock tower and I loved the soft light it cast on Lacie's face. Her long brown hair was still tucked back in a pony tail and her beautiful green eyes stood out in the dimmer light. As she stood next to me I looked at her, hiding my smile when she caught me staring. She was just the friend that I needed, and maybe it could be more.

Thoughts about Mom had been weighing most on my mind, but there were still some issues with Sarah. Talking with Lacie was a respite from it all.

I wondered if she could tell that I didn't want her to go now. Her car was across from my apartment so we started to walk to the corner.

"I really enjoy talking with you," I said. "I can't tell you how nice it is to talk with someone who's grounded in reality."

"I enjoy being with you too, Harry."

She put her arm around me and I instinctively put my arm across her shoulders. It felt as if she meant it as more than a friendly gesture. I didn't say anything, but looked down at her for a moment. Her head fit nicely in the top part of my arm. She looked up and smiled and we were silent as we walked the remaining way to the corner. I wondered what it would be like to be with someone again. Somehow, with Lacie it felt comfortable, although I was hardly sure of where this was going.

When we got to her car, she kept her hand on my side but turned to face me. Then she put her arms around my neck and kissed me. We both wanted it to last, and nothing mattered at all for that time. Wow! I was thrilled inside, but I tried to remain cool. Don't push too fast, I thought.

"I could really use some coffee. Do you have any, Harry?"

"I do," I said. "Just don't mind my place. It's a bit cluttered."

"I don't mind," she told me.

We crossed the street and went up to my apartment. I was happy that she wanted to spend more time with me. When we walked in, Lacie looked around for a moment, then went right over to the kitchen counter and filled the coffee pot.

"The coffee is in the left top cabinet, filters as well," I told her. "Just put in enough for you."

She could see that only the living room area was cluttered, but still clean. I just had nowhere else to put many of my things. I kept the kitchen, bathroom and bedroom organized. She started the coffee pot and then looked around. When Lacie stood by my bedroom door, I told her she should open it. I had a habit of making my bed every morning and I always kept my bedroom clean.

She turned back to the living room and back and forth once more, then laughed a little. She found my paradoxical room arrangements amusing. I was happy she recognized that I delimited the chaos. She mentioned that she noticed I mostly wore black clothes, so I told her to look in my closet. When she opened the closet door, she saw just about all black clothes inside. I explained how it was easy to decide what to wear each day and she smiled.

"What made you start wearing all black?" she asked.

I told her how in the past I had trouble matching colors and many times went out with unusual combinations. I thought it was fine, but some people I knew were not so kind with their comments.

"This way I didn't have trouble with that anymore," I said.

"You know, you're an unusual guy, Harry."

"I'm not quite sure how to take that, Lacie."

"I really like that about you," she said.

I could smell the coffee beginning to brew as Lacie walked around looking at my pictures and other things. She stopped at the shelf filled with items my girls had given me—paper and clay animals as well as other little things they made for me in school. She picked up each item and looked at it carefully, asking about the story that went with each. With all the clutter in the room, it was the only shelf that I left plenty of space on so I could easily see the items my girls made for me.

I cleared the coffee table as she continued to look around. She stopped at the telescope by the window.

"Do you take this out much?" she asked.

"Whenever I can," I explained.

I told her about how there was much more to look at from the back of the home Sarah and I owned in Salisbury Mills. The yard had a big open area surrounded at the edge by trees to block a good deal of the ambient light. It was darker than here in town, and in addition to the planets, the girls and I would look at star clusters, pulsars and even the galaxy Andromeda. Here in town, I had to settle for looking at just the planets. I told Lacie about a great spot in Sullivan County that I would love to take her to. There, the sky lit up with so many stars and the milky-way was a bright arch stretching from horizon to horizon.

"I would love to go," she said. "It sounds awesome."

Lacie asked me to tell her more about Malcolm and what happened to make him stop talking to me. I explained how it happened slowly, but started when I left college during the second semester of my second year. Malcolm felt as if I had abandoned him then. Of course that was never my intention, but I couldn't stomach the house anymore. By this time, Malcolm was able to avoid most confrontations with our father, but I began to yell back. We were too old for him to strike us and our father had mellowed enough with age anyway. He was limited to unimpressive tirades.

It was safe enough for Malcolm. He was 17 then and was entering college at the end of the year. He would spend more of his day in school and be working at night. Both of us always worked anywhere we could just to spend time away from the house, so we were able to pay for the college credits. But we couldn't afford the tuition and an apartment too.

Malcolm managed later to avoid the house even more, often staying with friends. I was a bit jealous of how effortlessly he was able to shelve his past, finish his degree, and how easily he made friends. I was never able to make friends as easily as Malcolm.

Since I left school, I was able to get enough work and overtime to cover my own needs so I tried to help my brother with a little extra money. I would drive around the richer neighborhoods on the nights they put out their trash, looking for old televisions that were discarded. People with money would often throw them out rather than invest the time needed to bring them for a simple repair. I was able to salvage about two out of three, selling them through classified ads in the Times Herald Record. I kept the money for the cost of the ad and gave the profits to Malcolm.

By the time Malcolm graduated, he removed what few possessions he had left from the house, and then never went back. He never called Mom, but he gave me the phone number for the first place he lived. When he moved from there he didn't give me his new number and never called me again. The only other time we spoke was my reaching out to him when our father died.

Then Lacie asked me to tell her more about Sarah and me.

We met at college in the beginning of my second year. Sarah left school shortly after I did, not completing her degree either. We soon got together again, and after awhile, got married. I worked hard and was able to earn enough to build a life for Sarah and myself. I did everything I could to buy our small home, working weekends and saving for the down payment. I did whatever I thought it took to be a good husband. Always loyal, I never expected life could be any other way.

When the girls were born, I thought we would be happier with each other. But when Sarah's parents moved to Westchester, she started to spend more time there. Her parents had a large home and made it more comfortable as time went on. After a few years, Sarah felt more at home there than with me. I went there a few times with her and the girls, but her parents always made me feel uncomfortable. We had problems, but what I couldn't understand was why Sarah never asked if we could go to counseling. Nonetheless, there was something missing long before that, I guess, making it not worth the effort.

Lacie poured her coffee and sat down next to me on the couch. It felt great to have someone to talk with, but Lacie understood me as well.

"What about you, Lacie? What do you see for yourself?"

I wanted to know everything about her.

"I'm happy," she told me. "Although I lost my mother, my Dad has always been there for me. I like my work at the center and I love helping my dad on the weekends at the tavern."

Lacie is a counselor at the Children's Assistance Center in Chester where she helps children with mental health problems and learning disabilities. I imagined that it would be difficult not to bring issues home with her, but she seemed to keep it in check. She only looked at the bright side.

I asked her to tell me more about the center and I saw the happiness in her eyes about the children she was able to help. She described each child with new energy, even in the cases that were far from resolved. She said that they were doing the best they could. It made me think about those who insist that everyone should pull themselves up by their bootstraps. But what they never seemed to realize is that some people don't have any bootstraps. Lacie told me about her friends and the fun they had in the clubs at the Newburgh marina. On the weekends she would meet them late at Pamela's on the Hudson, when she was done at the tavern. She told me the bands were great and things would just get started after midnight.

"Harry, you have to come to the clubs with me when things are better for you. I want so much for you to meet my girlfriends."

"It sounds great," I told her. "I would like that."

"So how is it at your job, Harry?" she asked.

I told her that I like it but want to go further, so I started to self-study and was working toward my network design certifications. I work pulling and terminating telecom and network wiring for a company out of Goshen. After sending money to Sarah and the girls, I have enough left over to keep me in this apartment until I could do better. I explained that once I was certified, I would be able to afford a larger apartment so my girls could have their own room when they stayed. I told her how good the owner of the company was. When he heard that my mother took a turn for the worse, he insisted I take the week as paid vacation time so I could be with Mom during her last days. It was so hard to study since Mom first became ill, but I only had two more courses and two more tests to go, when I was able to get back to it.

It had been hard to sleep lately anyway, so I wanted Lacie to stay a little longer. I wanted to hold her again.

I apologized for not having any food in the apartment and explained that, with visiting Mom so often now, I didn't have the time to go shopping. She told me not to worry, she was fine. Lacie asked if it would be OK for her to stay while she had one more cup. I told her that I wasn't going to see Mom until about eleven in the morning and I didn't expect

I would get too much sleep anyway. She poured her second cup and looked around at a few more things.

She stopped at my fossil collection and I told her the stories of how the girls and I spent hours at Black Rock, sometimes only to find one specimen. They were for the most part imprints in the rock of shelled animals called Brachiopods, and were found all over the area. There was no real value to them other than the memories they gave me with my girls. I pointed to a large microscope on the side table and explained how Kaela loved animals. So I collected pond water to show her animals she could never see with just her eyes.

"It's good that you involve your girls with science."

I told her I felt this country, this world, was so mired in myth that it stifled any real progress we could make for each other. With this much ignorance about science, my fear is that we'll leave our children a ruined planet.

"I do have hope, however slight," I told her.

Lacie understood.

"It would be a shame if dinosaurs lasted hundreds of millions of years and humans couldn't last ten million," I said.

I told Lacie how science has always been my passion: physics, astronomy, earth sciences, you name it. These are the subjects in which reality is evident to me. I'm outraged at the insistence from some that their opinions alone justified the placing of a disclaimer in school science books regarding evolution. It was pure religious blindness on the scale of when people believed the earth was flat. I felt more that they should put a disclaimer in their religious books. What I find most offensive, though, are those people who insist we should have dominion over the earth.

"What we need to be are caretakers," I said.

Lacie was looking into the microscope and there was a piece of Kaela's hair, still on the slide from another time the girls were over. All around the table were samples in slides, test tubes in a rack and electronics tools that I used to assemble little gadgets and make my repairs. What once took up a whole bench in my old garage workshop was now concentrated on that small table and few shelves above it. There were bins full of small parts I salvaged from old devices and rolls of different gauge wire. I watched Lacie as she examined the items on the table.

"What's this?" she asked.

She pointed to a large grey metal box with a long glass front panel and a dozen or so knobs and switches.

"That's an old ham radio that belongs to Billy, next door," I told her. "I'm waiting for one more part from the surplus electronics store."

I explained to her how, before Billy talked to me, his radio broke and Ben from the deli told me about it. Billy Ryan lost his leg a couple of years ago in the Iraq war and was on disability. The artificial leg he was fitted with caused him pain so it limited his walking. Ben told me the radio was what made his life bearable. He used it to speak to people, even a few vets like himself. He didn't have the money that he needed to have the shop repair it, so after Ben mentioned it, I approached Billy and offered to look at it.

"It's nice that you offered to do that for him," she said.

"Considering what he's sacrificed, it's nothing at all."

I felt so comfortable talking with Lacie. As I was staring at her, it got harder to hold my thoughts. She had that soft voice with a hint of a British accent, and when she touched me, I felt a shiver on the back of my neck.

"You're so cute, Lacie," I kind of blurted out when I meant to keep it to myself.

She smiled, but I still wondered if I should have said it. She came over and sat down again. This time she placed her hand on the side of my head and kissed me. It had been years since I felt passion from just a kiss, a feeling that left me years before Sarah moved out. It was like breathing again and I wondered how much she meant it. Lacie put her cup down, her head on my chest and squeezed me gently.

"You deserve to be happy, Harry."

"There are a few things I am going through now, but I will be," I told her. "Thank you, Lacie."

I want to be happy but there always seems to be something unexpected that comes up, something in the way to prevent it. Before Mom was ill, I was beginning to settle in and make the best of what I had, but her dying was bringing out uncomfortable memories.

With Lacie's head still on my chest, I was feeling calmer. So much so that I felt myself dozing off. I made a gesture to sit up so I would remain awake but she gently pushed me down.

"Relax, Harry. You look so tired."

Something about her was so soothing and a few minutes after lying back down, I fell asleep.

After about six hours of sleep, the light began to enter the window and it woke me. I felt Lacie lying next to me with one leg wrapped around me. She had removed her skirt and snuggled to fit on the couch. She's so beautiful. I stared at her legs up to her cute white underwear and I was happy she was there when I woke, happy that she felt this close to me. I held her tightly and stayed there for some time appreciating that it was possible to be close with someone again. Lacie was giving that to me.

There was some guilt, feeling good about her. Mom was ill and dying, but Lacie was someone I could turn to now. I could feel that. I closed my eyes and kissed her gently on her forehead, careful not to wake her.

I pulled back slightly to look at her face and I saw her slight smile as she slept. I put my hand on her back and kissed her head again.

I stayed with her a while but just couldn't sleep anymore. I slipped off the couch and covered Lacie with a small blanket I took from the closet near the bathroom. I got new clothes and went into the bathroom to shower. As I shaved, I thought about what kind of day it would be.

I was being dragged along like an unwilling participant engaged purely out of obligation. I never thought I'd have to see Mom suffer. She's only a couple of years shy of sixty and it shouldn't be time for her to go yet. I remember the first time I noticed Mom starting to look old. It brought a unique sadness. I was convinced that all those years of abuse by my father had slowly worn her down.

Even after my father died, the habits that she retained showed that she still felt anxious if she didn't comply with the absurd standards he insisted on when he was alive. That combined with her feelings of loss and guilt about Malcolm, I believe caused the stress which aided the progress of the cancer on her brain. Again I felt angry at Malcolm for going away. Mom was guilty of nothing but not leaving our father as the abuse was growing. She was as frightened of him as we were.

I was stepping into the shower and I heard the birds out back. The bathroom window looked out over the paved area behind the stores, and it was always quiet on Sundays. On other days, I could hear the store owners drive in and pull into their spaces.

The water felt good and I stayed in longer than usual. I knew that I was attempting to prolong getting out by washing over and over, so I thought I'd better stop. I finally did get out and dried off to get dressed. I was in for a difficult day so I dressed in comfortable jeans, a soft shirt and comfortable shoes. On weekends I was maybe not so diligent about shaving, wearing aftershave and the like. With Lacie now, I had a renewed sense of wanting to care about how I looked. After I dried my hair, I took one last look in the mirror and went into the living room.

When I looked at the couch I saw Lacie had gone. The small blanket was folded and had a note on top. I picked up the paper to read it.

> "Harry, I had to get home to shower and change.
> I promised to meet my friends for breakfast.
> I had a fantastic time being with you last night. I know
> you are going through so much so if you need a friend,
> call me, Lacie."

Her number was at the bottom.

I brewed some coffee and pulled a bagel out of the freezer. She had cleaned the coffee pot and I could see her cup from last night, washed and placed on the dish rack to dry. I looked out the front window at the spot where Lacie had been parked last night to see that her car was gone, although I knew it would be. I stared for a moment at the spot across the street where she kissed me for the first time.

After I put her number in my cell phone list, I emptied one of the small drawers on my desk and placed the note inside. I hoped it would be the first of many from her. I told the weekend nurse I would be there at eleven so I put some news on the television and relaxed for the moment with my breakfast. The first cup of coffee in the morning always tasted so good. My thoughts drifted off to Lacie, conversations, the way she looked and what she wore last night.

The house I grew up in was just about five miles down the road on the outskirts of Monroe, so I waited until almost a quarter to eleven and then walked down the stairs. When I stepped outside it was a beautiful day. I felt guilty for a moment, as if I could just not go, and I might spend the day at the park instead. I heard the door open from the stairs that led to the apartment above the deli and saw Billy walking out.

"Good morning, Billy."

He looked both ways down the road and then looked at me.

"I like coming out on Sundays. It's quieter then," he said.

Although most of the shops were closed Sunday, I hardly thought any day in the town center was anything but quiet.

"I guess it is," I told him.

"I like to pick up the Sunday paper from the bakery down the road," he said.

I mentioned that I was going in that direction and would be happy to give him a lift.

"That's nice of you, Harry, but it gives me a chance to exercise my good leg."

"I understand," I said. "By the way, I should have that radio back to you soon. I'm just waiting for one last part to be delivered."

"That's great, Harry, I really appreciate you fixing it. I didn't realize how much it meant to me until it was broken."

Ben told me Billy was saving for a new radio, but was only able to put away a few dollars each month. He hadn't saved enough to even repair the old one and if he did, it would've wiped out what he had saved toward getting his new one. It was obvious to me that he felt alone without it. I watched as he walked away struggling proudly. He lost his leg while fighting in Iraq and had so much trouble being fitted properly with his artificial one. It made me feel as if anything I went through in my life could never compare to what he experienced.

Before I talked with Billy for the first time, I thought he looked lost. He avoided talking to me as he did most everyone else, until I offered to fix his radio. Now at least I knew he had friends on the air, but I could see he was still worried that I might not be able to repair it. Almost finished, I knew it would work, but Billy wouldn't totally believe it until he saw for himself.

I got in my car and drove toward Monroe, passing Billy and the bakery soon after. The bakery was always packed after the church services let out nearby. Unlike the quieter surroundings in Washingtonville's town center, it filled as the people converged to buy their Sunday morning baked goods. I wondered how Billy dealt with the crowd.

There was something that felt different. I had been down this road so many times since I'd grown up, but for some reason today, I noticed the things that had changed, and I pictured what was there before they did. I had thoughts about riding my bike down this road as a child. Often riding to old man Perkowski's store for Mom, I memorized every crack in the sidewalk, every sign. The store was a tiny place with the door set right on a corner. There was a level above the store and, even with the couple of signs, it still looked more like a house.

He sold assorted groceries, and for years enjoyed a decent living, but as the strip malls went in, I could see the items on his shelf begin to collect dust. He would wipe off the dust with his apron before he put it in the bag. Mr. Perkowski died in the mid-eighties and the new owners converted the store back into living space. But lately, when I drive by, I can see the letters of old man Perkowski's sign bleeding through the now worn paint.

At least Mom's area had gone through so little change here at the outskirts of town. Trees were bigger and some of the older folks I could see were beginning to really show their age, but there had been modest growth on these streets. Unlike other neighborhoods, the wetlands confined building to a few small roads with houses.

I turned onto my old street and I could see Mom's house once I passed some of the largest trees that had grown into the road. From far away, it looked as it did while I was growing up, but as I got closer I could see neglect taking its toll. I did what I could when I could, but the old house was just too much to care for and I had my own house to maintain until Sarah left me.

Houses like Mom's weren't the type of homes which lasted forever. It was just a simple house and at this point unworthy of restoration. Light blue, with white trim, everything was dirty from years of wear. There was custom millwork on the porch that my grandfather made. You could tell it looked great when new, but my father never lifted a hand to maintain it.

When I parked outside, I saw that the nurse Grace had opened the shade and curtains so Mom could get some sunlight. Mom was finding it impossible to get around now, confined to her room. She could only make it to the bathroom on the other side of the chair by her bed, and then back. It made me a little uncomfortable being in Mom's room now. Until she was ill, I had avoided going in there since I moved out. Growing up, Malcolm and I felt safest in Mom's room, but now it brought back such bad memories of why we hid in there.

Chapter 4

When I got out of the car, I saw the curtains in John and Kathy Lowe's house pull back then let go again. They are a quiet couple and always keep to themselves. Ever since I can remember, they peeked out their windows whenever they heard any noise outside. Most of the children on my old street had grown and moved away, so it became more like a retirement community. They all knew that Mom wasn't doing well and to see a neighbor pass away had become a sad ritual followed by their attendance at the service. The neighbors were always there to make sure that not one of them left this earth without a respectable amount of mourners. To me that was a most profound and compassionate gesture.

I was staring at the peeling paint on the front of the house when Grace opened the door and stepped onto the front porch.

"Hello, Mr. Ladd. I have your mother in the chair this morning. I'm hoping the sunlight will do her some good."

"Thanks, Grace. Remember, please call me Harry."

"Thanks, Harry. Ms. Barnes told me she talked to you last night about your mother's delusions. It started yesterday and we thought it might be temporary. I'm sorry to say, but it doesn't seem as if she's doing any better today."

Grace told me Mom called her "Ruth," the same as she did Ms. Barnes. She said Mom worried that her husband would be angry if she didn't recover fast enough to care for his needs.

"I didn't correct her," she said. "I just didn't think it was worth frightening her by explaining things."

"I agree," I said. "I just want her to be comfortable".

"The doctor added a slight sedative in addition to her pain medication. It should help her feel calm."

"I appreciate your kindness toward Mom," I told her. "All of the nurses have been so good to us."

"Doctor Jabir was by earlier. He wanted me to tell you that just getting to the chair and bathroom would be more laborious for your mother now, and her breathing was becoming shallower because of the progression. He also wants you to know that there is nothing he can do about the delusions since they're caused by the cancer. He left his number, should you have any questions."

"Thank you, Grace. Please take some time for yourself. I'll bring my mother's lunch up and go sit with her."

When I stepped in from the porch, I heard the familiar creak in the floor about two feet inside. Grace went into the sitting room to read and I went past the stairs to the kitchen. I had been here so many times since I moved out, but somehow today it felt different. I could almost hear the conversations we had in this room, and Malcolm's voice as it once was. I remembered the frequent pounding of a fist on the table from our father when he was angered over the mere thought that we were disobeying him. The food would fly. Then he would leave the room so he wouldn't have to look at the mess he had caused. He waited for Mom to clean it up.

Malcolm would cower, so frightened by our father. But I had just stopped caring about anything that happened. It wasn't like there was anything we could do, anyway. Mom told me that our father wasn't always like that. He was nicer to her before they married, but as time went on, he changed. From time to time, he struggled to make ends meet and the stress seemed to boil him over.

Although most times he trucked containers only around the county, now and then he would get a load to haul down to Florida. Those times were a respite for Mom, Malcolm and me, giving us a few days with him away. He didn't drink often, but after a long haul he had enough cash for a night in the pub. We hoped he would pass out when he came home. If not, we had to worry that the alcohol might fuel him. Those times even frightened me.

Once in awhile, Mom couldn't help herself and she intervened when our father lost it. She made the mistake once of being in the way as my father went to strike me. While he normally limited his abuse of Mom to verbal tirades, this time without realizing, he pushed her so hard that she fell and pulled a muscle in her leg. She couldn't walk for days. I remembered wishing then that my father would be killed on the highway as he drove his rig. I pictured him in a fiery wreck, suffering horribly. I hated it when I thought like that.

Harry returned from Ruth's house and noticed his father's car was gone. He couldn't have felt more relieved. He went up to tell his mother that Ruth said she could come over in an hour. Rue was in bed, Malcolm rolled up next to her, and she was holding his head.

"Mom, I'm hungry," Malcolm said. "My food was thrown on the floor."

Rue was is in pain and knew she couldn't get up.

"Ruth will be over soon, sweetheart. I will ask her to make you something."

"I'll make something for Malcolm, Mom," Harry told her.

"I appreciate that, Harry. I heard your father's car. Did he leave?" Rue asked.

"Yes, and I hope he stays away."

They never spoke about what happened. Just as Rue couldn't help but clean up the mess as soon as she could, they always put Henry's outbursts out of mind just as fast. But seeing their mother hurt and in bed was a reminder that made it more difficult this time.

When Malcolm and Harry got to the kitchen, they saw everything had been picked up. There was a rectangular dark spot on the wall where the photograph of Rue's parents hung for so many years. It was darker in that spot because the picture had shielded the spot from the sunlight that faded the surrounding wall. The kitchen smelled like an old mop. Rue barely was able to rinse it because she had been in so much pain.

"Malcolm, would you like a sandwich?" Harry asked.

"If there's peanut butter," Malcolm told Harry, while looking down at the table.

All Malcolm did was to stare down at the table. He was feeling so hopeless.

Harry pulled out the jar and found it almost empty, but he managed to scrape enough out to make the sandwich for his little brother. It wasn't much, but it would have to do. Their mother always left money in the cabinet. Harry would ride his bike to old man Perkowski's store the next day to get more. When Malcolm sat down to eat, Harry stayed with him. He was listening to make sure their father didn't return before they could make it back upstairs to their room. They would run out the back door if he did.

"Harry," Malcolm said. "When I get old enough, I'm gonna run away. I don't like it here."

Harry didn't respond. Being older, he knew there was nothing they could do, but he felt bad for his little brother.

"Do you want something else to eat?" Harry asked him. "There are sweet pickles in the refrigerator."

"This is OK," Malcolm said. "Harry, do you think Mom will be OK next week for my graduation?"

"I hope so Malcolm, but I'll be there."

When Malcolm finished, Harry checked down the hall and they ran up the stairs. At the top, Harry noticed a glow beneath his mother's door, so he went to check on her. He opened the door but saw nothing unusual. Rue was sleeping with her head turned slightly away. The boys could stay in their room now. Ruth would just walk in when she saw Henry's car was gone.

I heated some soup and made a small sandwich which I placed on a large tray to bring up to Mom. The bedroom I had shared with Malcolm was just at the top of the stairs, so I walked in for a moment to look around. The room was mostly cleared now, with a few boxes stored there since we left. There was a yellowing flyer still pinned to the wall where Malcolm's bed used to be. It was for a school talent show during Malcolm's senior high school year. He and two friends had entered as a singing trio. I can't remember the song but I can remember the way they butchered it. Our father wouldn't let Mom attend because he wouldn't stand for losing her service. He considered the show unimportant. I remembered how much that hurt Malcolm. But I went to his show.

I shut the door behind me as I walked out.

The hall had become dingy and weathered with a smell of old paint and old wood. The wooden floor was marred in the center all the way to Mom's door and the shellac on the baseboard had yellowed with age. Part of me always felt guilty that things had gotten so bad, but long before I was able to help, the need for maintenance had already gotten out of hand. Neither of us had enough money for all the supplies needed anyway.

I could hear Mom shuffling some belongings as I slowly pushed open the door with my free hand. She was sitting in the chair next to the bed and I could see a look of worry on her face. I startled her slightly when she saw me.

"Hello, Harry," she said. "I know your father won't be happy if I can't get his clothes done soon."

"Don't worry, Mom," I said. "He's not around right now."

I told her that he had gotten a container to haul down to Florida. I thought it might give her some relief to think he'd be gone for a few days.

"Did you help Malcolm make something to eat? You know how he forgets to eat if I don't help him."

"I helped him," I said.

"Why aren't you out playing, Harry?"

I told her that I wanted to stay home to make sure she was OK. It felt very strange to play along with Mom, but I saw no reason to confuse her by trying to explain. I was relieved that Mom wasn't frightened by my older appearance. Just as she thought the nurse was her neighbor, Ruth, she evidently saw me as she did then. It was a bit disturbing at first, but there was nothing I could do, so I just went along.

"I'm sorry that I'm not well enough to get around right now. You must be hungry for a good meal," she said.

"I'm OK, Mom. I've eaten already and I even brought you some lunch."

"Oh, thank you, Harry."

I pulled over the small side table next to her chair and placed the tray down. She smelled the soup and started to eat her sandwich. I sat in a chair by the window and watched her as she ate her little meal. I wanted to tell her I would miss her and how it hurt to watch her suffer from her illness, but she no longer understood what was happening to her. She looked so pale and it was hard to watch her getting progressively worse.

"Ruth has been coming by often," she said. "She's a good neighbor."

"Yes, she is," I told her.

"She had a doctor stop by to check on me, but I told him I was OK. He gave me something for the pain."

"I'm glad he did," I said.

"I could hear her straightening up downstairs earlier. Please give her some of the money from the cupboard for the groceries she picked up. You know where I keep it."

"I'll make sure she gets it," I told her.

I could see that the sedative was making her slightly groggy. She drifted off as she was eating, paying little attention to anything more. I looked out the window until she was done. Mom was too young to have this illness take her. She wasn't even sixty. My girls should have had more time with their grandmother. Just what about Mom's suffering was part of any grand plan? People live and people die, that's just how it is. How absurd life is when you think about it.

Mom finished, so I took the tray and table away and pulled my chair over near hers. She was looking at me proudly, but with almost a look of embarrassment, as if she herself was somehow to blame for her condition.

"Mom, I love you," I told her. "I wish you were well."

"I love you too, Harry. You are growing up to be a fine young man. I'm sorry that your father was rough on you."

"It's OK, Mom. I understand."

"I'm worried about Malcolm though, she said. You can see that it's harder on him. I only wish that I could do something."

"You are doing the best that you can, Mom. I don't blame you at all."

It was funny how being around Mom always made me feel like a kid. But now that she saw me as one, it was eerie. I couldn't help but think that her mind had caused her delusions to protect her from the memories of everything that would one day break her heart. What hurt me most was that I couldn't call the girls now for them to say their goodbyes. To her, they weren't even born yet.

She started to get up to use the bathroom and I went over to help her to her feet. I noticed that she had a limp and was holding her right leg. I wondered if she might have fallen when she was alone.

"Mom, Is your leg OK?" I asked.

"It hurts a little," she said. "I'll be alright. Harry, you don't need to stay with me. You should go out and play."

"No, Mom," I said. "I would like to stay with you for awhile if it's OK."

"I just don't want to burden you, but can you make sure Malcolm has something to eat when he gets home?"

I had to think of something so she wouldn't worry about him.

"Don't you remember?" I said. "Malcolm is staying over Daniel's house so they can study."

Daniel was Malcolm's best friend through elementary and middle schools.

"I didn't. But please make sure he is taken care of," she said.

"Don't worry, Mom. I will call over to check on him later."

Mom shut the door and I waited as it took quite awhile for her to finish. After about 10 minutes, I called in.

"Mom, is everything alright?"

"Yes Harry, I will be out in a minute."

Mom was dying and I thought it a little silly to worry about her now. It was just a protective reaction. What could happen to her, worse than what already has? I heard the water and some footsteps. Then she came out and sat down in the chair. She used her hands to help position her right leg.

"I'm going to take the tray down to the kitchen," I told her. "Can I get you anything else?"

"No. Thank you, Harry."

I told her I would be right back and I took the tray down. I felt relieved for a moment to be able to leave the room. A couple days ago when I was here, she was still Mom. Now she had lost decades of her life and I could only hope she wouldn't lose any more.

Grace heard me come down the stairs, so she walked into the hall.

"How is she doing?" she asked.

"She's fine," I told her. "I noticed she had some pain in her right leg."

"I forgot to mention it. We noticed that as well. The doctor said there were no bruises when he looked it over and he doesn't see anything wrong. He thought it was unusual, given the pain medication she's on, but he increased the dose a bit."

Grace was genuinely kind. It took a unique person to repeatedly comfort families while she tended to her patients during their last days.

"Your Mom has been speaking about another son, Malcolm. Will he be coming to visit her?" she asked.

I explained to her how Malcolm left years ago and wanted nothing to do with us. I didn't tell her the details, but she still had a look of disapproval on her face about a son who wouldn't come see his dying mother.

"Does he know how badly your mom is doing now?" she asked.

I told her that he wouldn't care and how he refused to come to our father's funeral when Mom needed him there. I explained a little bit about our father and his temper. How Malcolm and I both hated him, but that my brother blamed Mom as well.

"Well, at a time like this you would think that he could set aside his anger," she said.

Grace told me a story of regret in her life that she could never forget. How her good friend Alva was suffering from depression. How the friend drove off the road one night and was killed. Grace wasn't so sure Alva didn't mean for it to happen. She felt guilty she hadn't realized how bad the problem was until it was too late.

"I should have seen the signs when she became depressed," she told me. "I should have noticed when she was changing for the worst. She was such a good friend and I trusted her when she told me things would be OK."

I never said it, but I couldn't see where Grace was at fault. The conversation still made me feel guilty, though, that I hadn't gotten word to Malcolm. Here I was feeling guilt when he never cared to keep in touch. Where were his feelings of regret about Mom? What made him so set in his ways?

I took the tray to the kitchen and put some ice and water into a pitcher to bring to Mom. As I reached into the cabinet to get a glass, I remembered pushing a chair up to the counter to reach the glasses as a child. Things I had done a thousand times since then, but now were bringing back memories. A couple of tears came, but I quickly changed my thoughts. I didn't want Mom to see me feeling sad or ask too many questions, so I took a few moments before I went back upstairs.

"Mom, I brought some ice water should you get thirsty."

"Thanks Harry, I would like some now."

I poured her a glass and sat back in the chair near hers. She had that worried look on her face again and I wondered what she was thinking.

"I'm sorry I couldn't help you, Harry, when your father lost his temper."

"I told you Mom, I don't blame you for anything."

"But will Malcolm? He's so afraid and it makes me feel helpless."

There wasn't much I could say since she didn't remember that Malcolm would abandon her someday.

"I understand Mom, but what could you do?"

"If only I had the courage, I would tell your father to leave," she said.

"So why do you stay with him, Mom?"

I know I probably shouldn't have asked, but I was interested nonetheless.

"I don't know how we would get by. What would we have?" she asked.

"Mom, we always have each other."

In the past, I never heard my mother talk like this. Maybe if I had had the wisdom to listen then, I could have helped her through those times. As a kid I stormed out, leaving Mom alone to deal with our father. Now I have the insight of being older and knowing what was coming. So much of what she felt, I had never realized.

"Mom, I know that you are only doing what you believe is best for Malcolm and me. I wish that he wouldn't hurt you so much. It doesn't help for you to think about this right now."

"Harry, I can hardly believe you're only twelve. You're such a wise young man."

I knew now the year Mom believed it to be. She said I was twelve, so Malcolm was only ten, and I thought about how torn she was that year. I wish there was something I could do to comfort her. At least she had forgotten all of the bad things to come later in her life.

"Whatever you want, Mom, I'll support you," I said.

"Thanks, Harry. I needed to hear that."

She was crying a little, but she didn't want me to see. When Malcolm and I were kids we heard her crying many times when she thought we weren't around, but almost never when we were there. Only in a profoundly emotional moment would Mom or I shed a tear in front of anyone else, but it was even more uncomfortable to see each other cry. Malcolm always cried easily.

"Things will get better soon, Mom," I told her.

But not in the way that Mom thought. In death, there is no pain. I hated lying to her, but why should she go through all this anguish without feeling the least bit of hope? I wanted her to have someone to talk with this time and I understood now how alone and helpless she must have felt.

When I was twelve, I never cared about Mom. I was selfish then and so angry at my father. I was grateful Mom taught me later that I could change. With any positive change always comes regret. If you can't see the things you do that are wrong, what hope would you have to change them?

I talked with Mom for hours about times in the past she recalled as if they were yesterday. When she dwelled on my father, I tried repeatedly to steer the conversation toward the more pleasant moments. It was hard to remember everything that happened back then, but I did my best. I was starting to make her smile and she was happy for a time.

"I really like when you take us to Black Rock," I told her.

Just as I take my girls, Mom took Malcolm and me to hike in Black Rock Forest.

"We'll go again when I'm better," she told me.

This was one of the conversations that made Mom smile. Hiking to the top, we felt far removed from our problems. There was so much space for so few people. You could hike all day and see only one or two others. Up on the trails, Malcolm and I could laugh and not feel as if we would be pounced on. Nothing could touch us up there. It was where we had our happiest memories and the reason I was creating new ones there with my girls. Trying to keep Mom happy with the best parts of the past was therapeutic for both of us, and it made me feel a bit more comfortable with her regression now.

The conversation itself made Mom tired and she fell asleep once again. It was only half past three so I waited, hoping we could still have a little more time before she had supper. It was only a short while until I began dozing off as well. I'd part my eyelids from time to time, to see if Mom had awakened.

In a moment, only half awake I saw a light on Mom's wall. It surrounded the picture of her parents, but, strangely, I saw no reflection on the glass. I was compelled to find out where it was coming from so I walked over to the picture and waved my hand in front, attempting to block the light. I made no shadow. It couldn't be coming from the wall behind, but I tilted the picture up nonetheless to look. But before I could raise the frame enough to peek behind, the light faded. What the hell was that? I sat back in the chair again hoping it would happen again and give me another chance to find out.

A short time later Mom woke and she still seemed happy. It made me feel good that I could comfort her after all. She remained awake for the rest of my visit, but it was almost time for her to eat. I got up and kissed her on the forehead.

"Mom, Ruth told me she would be bringing you supper. I'm going to go now."

"OK, Harry. Thanks for spending so much time with me today. It was nice to talk. Please don't forget to check on Malcolm."

"I won't forget," I said. "I hope you can rest now Mom."

I walked down to the sitting room just at the bottom of the stairs. Grace would normally get off at four o'clock, but today she was staying a couple of extra hours.

"How was your visit?" she asked.

"I believe I kept her happy today," I told her. "It was a good day."

"After she eats, I will help her into bed. I'll also make sure the evening nurse knows to call you, should her condition change," she told me.

"Thank you, Grace."

I pushed open the door and went down the front walk to my car. Behind the wheel, I just sat there thinking for a moment, when through the windshield I saw Mike Ferguson coming up the street. He's an elderly neighbor who had been concerned about Mom. I could tell he wanted to speak so I stepped out and shook his hand.

"Hello, Mike."

"Hi, Harry. I wanted to ask you how Rue is doing."

"I'm sorry, Mike. The doctor believes she has just a few days," I told him.

"I'm sorry for you, Harry."

"I appreciate that," I said. "I wish you could visit with her, but she's not herself now."

"I understand," he told me. "Everyone was asking about her now that she doesn't come out. She's a good woman, your mom."

"She tries her best," I told him. "See you soon, Mike."

It was nice to know that after our father died, Mom was able to make a few acquaintances in the neighborhood, although just in the most casual sense.

I got back into my car, and driving home, I dwelled on mixed feelings from my visit.

Chapter 5

Although I needed something to eat, I passed right by the supermarket on my way home. I just wasn't up to going in there. The deli was closed on Sunday, but I could always get something to eat at Brooks. I could stop in and get something to take out.

Seeing Mom disoriented today was incredibly sad. It brought back some bad memories, but at least there were some good ones as well. I grew angrier at Malcolm because it was hard not to feel guilty that I hadn't called him. I was certain he didn't care. He never cared, so why should I bother? Would it be wrong not to give him a final chance to make peace with her? I just didn't know, but I refuse to keep thinking about it right now.

I walked into my apartment and threw my keys and cell on the counter just inside the door. I noticed the light blinking on the phone recorder so I pressed the button to retrieve the message.

"Hi, Harry, it's Lacie. I know you've had a tough day so if you want to talk, call me. I enjoyed being with you last night."

I was happy to hear her voice and I wanted to be with her. I was glad there was still someone who might be right for me. All those years with Sarah and not once did I feel this way. Sarah and I grew comfortable hoping that the other would change, but neither of us did.

I pulled the note from the drawer and pressed in the number.

"Hello," Lacie said.

"Hi, Lacie, it's me, Harry."

"Hi Harry. I'm so glad you called. How was your visit? How is your Mom?"

"I think I was able to keep her happy today. As sick as she is, I believe we had a good day."

"I'm glad," she said. "Would you like some company?"

"I really would," I said. "I would love to see you."

"Me too," she said. "I can be there in about forty-five minutes or so."

"I'll see you then," I told her.

Although I already had taken a shower this morning, I felt that a nice one now would help me feel better. I got some clean clothes and went into the bathroom. I wanted to look nice for Lacie. I wanted to be with her. It helped me so much right now.

Unlike this morning, I only took a quick shower. I was eager to get dressed so I could straighten up a bit before Lacie got here. Careful to wear better clothes, black, but less worn. I quickly put away items where I could and gave the kitchen and bathroom a quick cleanup.

When I finished straightening up, I thought I would spend a few minutes working on Billy's radio. He was anxious to get it back so I wanted to finish soldering the board connections before the part I ordered arrived. Most people reached out now through the Internet, but the short wave radio was where Billy's friends were. I knew how lonely he was feeling without it. His radio was a little easier to repair because it was a bit older than most. Just about all electronic devices today were constructed with solid state circuit boards. They're no longer able to be repaired in the old sense. Instead, entire boards are discarded and replaced.

I never had formal training, but years ago I started to read books on electronics and realized I had a knack for it. With the Internet, it was easy to find all the parts I needed and all the schematics as well. Most people who lived around here were not very well off so, when they found out I could fix things, I had a manageable amount of items coming my way. Some I could fix, while others I couldn't. But I could at least save them the bench charge it would take to tell them when it was not able to be repaired.

I kept my laptop on a small desk next to my work table, just large enough for it and my small printer. For Internet, I connected to the wireless network from the computer store. The owner Hewitt threw in the access as part of the rent. I hadn't checked email since Friday, so I took a few minutes to go online. When I opened my email program, I watched a steady stream of spam come in.

I heard a knock on the door, and when I opened it, I saw Lacie holding two brown paper bags with handles.

"Adams," she said. "I thought you could use some things."

She put the cold items in the refrigerator and emptied the rest of the things onto the counter. She opened the cabinets to see how they were arranged, in order to put the rest of the groceries away. There were pasta, sauce, cold cuts, bread and some other items she guessed I might like. Adams Fairacre Farms was the best place in the area to get fresh groceries and I knew she went out of her way to stop there.

"Thanks, Lacie. I'd been meaning to get some things."

"Did you eat yet?" she asked.

"I was going to pick something up at your Dad's place."

"Well, I'll make something for us."

She put on a large pot of water for pasta and some sauce on a low heat. I asked if she would like coffee and she said yes, so I started a small pot.

I felt like kissing her, so I did. I didn't want to wait anymore. We stood there and I held her until the water boiled.

"Let me get the pasta," she said.

I poured two cups of coffee and brought them over to the couch. Lacie put in the pasta and came over to sit with me.

"So tell me about your visit," she said.

"Mom's living in the past, Lacie. It must be from the final stages of her brain cancer. Mom said she couldn't believe that I was only twelve. She sees me that way and I didn't want to frighten her. I made up stories about where Malcolm and our father were when she asked about them. She's talking to me about all her regrets, things I'd never heard before. I was only twelve and never listened then, but at least I can listen and comfort her now."

"That has to be tough, Harry."

"As disturbing as it first was to see her like that, something made me think it was good that she didn't know what she was really going through. She knows she's not well, but thinks it's just a passing illness. I'm happy that she sees the nurses as her old friend Ruth."

Lacie got up a few times to stir the pasta and the sauce. She bought the sauce that Adams sold made with local tomatoes and it smelled great. I set up mats, forks and napkins on the coffee table by the couch. I told her I appreciated the company, and the groceries.

"I knew you wouldn't be up to stopping for food, and besides I thought you could use a friend," she said.

"I can use a friend, Lacie, Thanks."

While we ate, we glanced at each other from time to time. Whether we were talking or just staying silent, it felt nice to be with her. I was increasingly feeling that Lacie was good for me.

When we finished, she put the dishes in the sink to wash them.

"Harry, let's go for a walk. You could use some fresh air," she said.

"That sounds good," I told her. "Let me get a light shirt to go over this."

As we walked down the stairs to the street, the bottom door opened and Pico came in carrying a pie. Pico lived with his wife Belita just a few houses down. I was in their home for the first time just a week ago. Pico snapped off the end of his cable connection and I stopped in to fix it. They had a tiny home, but it was fine since it was just the two of them. They had simple things. Not much in the way of luxuries, but a whole wall in their living room was covered in religious symbols, prayers framed and a crucifix. Pico said it was Belita's ticket to heaven. They're a cute couple.

"Harry, oh and hi, Lacie," he said. "It's nice to see you. How's your father?" he asked Lacie.

"Great Pico, he's doing well."

"Harry, I'm glad I caught you. Belita wanted to thank you for fixing her blender. She made this pie for you. I want to thank you for fixing our cable connection as well."

"That's OK, Pico. I was happy I could help."

"Without the television, it was too quiet in the house," he said. "I hate the quiet."

"Please thank her for the pie," I told him.

"It's apple. Not Hodges apples but still good. She said that she'll make you more with local apples when they're in season."

The pie was still warm and I could smell it from the moment Pico stepped into the doorway.

"It smells fantastic to me, Pico."

Lacie asked for my key and took the pie up into the apartment while I walked Pico out the bottom door.

"I see you are keeping company with Brice's daughter. She is a beautiful young lady. A kind soul," he said.

"I really enjoy being with her," I told him.

"Be good to her Harry, she's worth holding on to," he said.

"I will."

"Ben told me how ill your mom is now. I'm sorry to hear it."

"Thanks Pico. We're just trying to keep her comfortable now."

"Well, I wish you the best, Harry, and thanks again for your help."

Pico started to walk back to his house.

"Please give my best to Belita," I said. "And please thank her for the pie."

"I will. Bye, Harry."

Lacie came out and we walked down Route 94 away from the town center toward Salisbury Mills. She put her arm around my waist and I put mine around her shoulder. Just beyond the row of stores, the road was filled with small neighborhood houses and a few back roads. There were sidewalks for some distance on 94 but on the side streets there were none. We walked by the side of the road. Then we found a tiny road bridge by a small stream and watched the water for awhile.

"You know, it's nice what you do for the people around here," Lacie told me.

"It's nothing, I said. People around here don't have much. They don't have enough sometimes to replace things or the money to have someone repair the things that break."

"Not many people can do those things and even fewer would take the time to help their neighbors like that."

"I do it when I get time and they're willing to wait. It's no trouble really."

"So how did you learn to repair things?" Lacie asked.

"When I was still a teenager I just started to read about electronics and couldn't get enough. After that, I found it easy to fix my own things. Simple electrical devices were even easier."

We walked around the back streets for awhile and the evening air felt great. From the street furthest back, we could see the Moodna Valley and Schunemunk Mountain. It was so awesome. The end of this road bordered on some of the valley wetlands and, being close to twilight, there was a symphony of crickets and frogs. The sounds of spring were so loud but still relaxing. We sat on a large tree that had fallen by the side of the road, looking into the valley and talking about some of the neighborhood people.

"You know, Harry, I've gotten to know many of the people around here because they stop in the tavern every now and then. Many of them never talked to each other before. Lately, I do see them talking. Since you know them all, they feel as if they now have a common friend in you," Lacie said.

"I guess I'm making up for a bad start," I said. "When I was young I had a hard time making friends. I felt if I couldn't talk to someone with more depth than the game scores or the weather, then I would rather be alone. When I grew up, I learned that I expected too much from people. It wasn't fair to fault them for wanting to start with casual conversation. The depth would come out when they felt comfortable enough with me. I found there's something worth knowing about most people if you take the time to find it. No matter how well off or not someone is, or how intelligent, all of us feel the same joys or pains of life. Still, when it comes to someone I could love, I need more. I need someone like you, Lacie. I need a best friend."

She hugged me, and I knew she was ready to hear that. Lacie got up and sat backwards on my lap, her chest toward mine. She put her arms around my neck and I leaned back at times so we could look at each other. She fit so well when I held her. Her skin was soft and she smelled nice. I could tell that she wanted to look good for me, as I did for her. I don't believe in fate but I felt fortunate to have met her and hoped that she felt the same. I was really starting to love her.

Just a week ago I couldn't have imagined falling in love again. I felt resigned to being alone out of fear that if I met someone, she would end up leaving me as Sarah did. It felt different with Lacie. She was caring and open. She made me feel as if there wasn't anything wrong with me that made Sarah leave, but that we just weren't right for each other. I could see that now.

It felt so great to hold her. I squeezed her tighter, wishing she would never let me go, and I wondered if I really deserved this. I could have stayed here with her all evening, but after awhile it was completely dark so we decided to go back into town. There are no streetlamps on the side roads. The only light we had came from the porch lamps and light posts of the homes we passed.

We took it slow going back. It was so nice out, and there were only so many nights like this during the year. It was perfect. Lacie asked if we could walk along the stores, so we started walking toward the library, stopping to look into all the windows. All the window displays were interesting, but I especially loved looking in the window at Hewitt's. All the technology in the front window excited me, just as the window of a toy store did as a kid. I thought that the display window in the auto parts store up ahead gave the same feeling to others, but it had always been of little interest to me. As we got closer to the corner, we could hear music playing in The Basement Bar, appropriately named since it was in the basement beneath the stores.

"Come on, Harry. I'll buy you a drink. Let's stop in for a short time."

She took me by the hand and pulled me into the bar.

The bar's entrance was between the auto parts store and the deli. Walking down there were three-foot-wide wooden steps between walls made of brick. The place was a renovated old basement with columns throughout, a dozen small tables and a little corner platform. It had a piano and was just large enough to seat two more instrumentalists. On one of the large walls there was a big neon sign which read "JAZZ" and in the back was the bar, just wide enough for six stools.

The music was acoustic with a trio playing. There was piano, acoustic guitar and standup bass. They were playing Night Train and were quite good. It was obvious they had been a trio for some time because every part of the song was tight. It was a good rendition of the song, but I still missed the horn. This place was popular enough to fill, yet remained a well-kept secret. Most of the people who did come were repeat customers who enjoyed the music on the weekends. The regulars were an odd bunch, though, a kind of modern day version of beatniks. Most ignored everyone else, so they were easy to be around.

We eyed a table in the back and Lacie told me to go sit down while she went up to get us something to drink.

"How about some wine?" she asked.

"I'll leave it to you," I told her.

I sat down and stared at Lacie as she stood at the bar. It was cute how she rose up on the tips of her toes, leaning far enough to order our wine. Lacie is petite, but her body is so well-proportioned for her size. She bought us both a glass of Beringer, White Zinfandel, and came over.

"This place always makes me feel comfortable," she said.

"I'm glad you came by and got me out of the apartment for awhile," I told her. "It helps a lot."

"Besides the fact that I enjoy being with you, you're worth it, Harry," she said.

I thought of how Sarah looked at me as somewhat of a failure, because I hadn't advanced as quickly as she wanted. It was clear after she left, that the things I tried to do for us mattered very little. I put in so much overtime that it was hard to study for my certifications. We grew far more concerned with the logistics of life than with caring about each other.

"I'm glad you started coming into Dad's place, Harry. I liked you since the first time we talked."

"I never knew," I told her.

"You weren't looking," she said. "For a long time, I could see you were still hurt from what happened with Sarah. Last night, when you finally asked if we could go out some time, I wasn't going to let it go."

"I'm glad you didn't," I said. "I was beginning to think I had nothing left to offer anyone."

"It was Sarah who made you feel that way. Everyone who knows you can see how much you care about the things that really matter. You are unique, Harry."

She made me feel I had value again. With everything I'd been through this year, it was easy to lose confidence. We listened to the music for a while but I knew Lacie had work in the morning. When we finished the wine, I reminded her.

"Lace, you have to get up early. We better get going."

"I know. Thanks, she said. I just hate to leave you now."

"Me, too," I said.

Now when she was with me I didn't want her to go either, so we walked to my apartment even slower this time. Lacie was parked right outside and we stood in the doorway to hold each other.

"I want to come up for a moment," she said.

How could I say no? I didn't want to say no. We went upstairs and Lacie placed the pie in the refrigerator now that it had long cooled. Mom had very little time and I asked Lacie if it would be too much to ask her to be with me during the service and funeral. She said there would be no way now that I would have to go through it alone. She told me she would be with me through it all. I explained how Sarah was prepared to bring the girls for the funeral when the time came. I wish the girls could meet Lacie under better circumstances, but there just wouldn't be enough time for that now.

"I know the girls will like you," I told her. "They want me to be happy."

"Some time in the future, once things settle down, we can take the girls out together," she said.

"That would be great," I told her.

It was getting late, so I reminded Lacie again that she needed to get up for work.

"Do you have an alarm clock?" she asked.

"Well, sure, I do. Why?" I asked.

"I want to stay with you tonight, Harry," she said quietly. "Do you want me to?"

"Yes," I told her. "I do."

"I can leave early enough to stop at my place and get ready before work."

She asked me to set the alarm to seven thirty, which I did. I handed Lacie a set of towels, a new toothbrush and an extra robe from the closet. She let me get ready first as we took turns washing up for bed. When Lacie came out of the bathroom, I could see that the robe was a bit large.

"I realize the robe doesn't fit so well."

"It will do fine," she told me.

She looked so beautiful to me, in the oversized robe with arms folded up and bottom to the floor. She took my hand and we went into my bedroom. We barely talked anymore but made love for some time and fell asleep holding each other.

Chapter 6

I started to hear the muffled low sounds of early morning when I opened my eyes. Lacie had already gone home to get ready for work. I wished that I were going to work as well. I wanted things to get back to normal, but it was a selfish thought. Everyone has pain to deal with.

There was a note on my night table.

"Harry, I hope you're OK today."
"Call me when you get home.... Love, Lacie."

For a moment I had to convince myself that last night happened. It was the first time I felt no doubt. I knew she loved me and I felt the same way about her.

It was still much too early to leave for Mom's. Most weekdays, Nurse Maia would be there, taking her out of bed as they did each day, just after her morning routine. I planned to go at eleven so I made the bed, put on some coffee and jumped into the shower. Even with the sadness about Mom, another part of me felt good because of what was happening with Lacie. Thoughts of being alone were gone. It made me realize that even if Sarah and I had stayed together, I would still have ended up feeling essentially alone.

After showering, I was just putting my clothes on when the doorbell rang. People who knew me would just walk up and knock on the top door, so I looked out the window to see who it was. There was a delivery truck parked out front. I went down to answer the door. I knew it was the part I ordered for Billy's radio. It was a benefit to live by the stores because deliveries always came early. I signed for the small box and brought it upstairs. There was still time before going to see Mom, so I opened the box and decided to finish repairing the radio. It wouldn't take long and I knew that Billy was in need of a decent break.

The coffee smelled great as I poured a cup. The first coffee of the morning, I would always make stronger. It was just what I needed.

I plugged in the soldering iron and opened the little container of flux. All the other steps of the repair had already been completed, so I needed only to remove the old part and solder in the new one. Once the iron was hot, I soldered the new part in place and then let the joints cool. I turned on the power switch, the radio lit and after a moment of warming up I could hear some conversations when I turned the channel dial. Billy had given me a small antenna for testing. Once he hooked it back up to the one on the roof, he would be good to go.

I left it on for a while to make sure that it was burned-in and went to pour myself another cup of coffee. Lacie had brought some fresh bagels with the other groceries last night, so I cut one to eat. Adams bagels were just about the closest tasting to the ones you could buy in Manhattan. Going out of her way to buy them there showed the extra care she took.

I heard the cars out back as the store owners pulled in to park and open their stores. Ben would already be in his store. He always opened at seven a.m. sharp, but the others started pulling in any time after eight thirty, ready to open at nine.

Billy was often out on the street early, so when I finished eating, I packed up his radio. I was hoping he was home so I could give it to him before leaving for Mom's house. As I stepped out, I saw Hewitt unlocking his front door for business. Hewitt bought the building a few years ago and was running a PC repair business which made him a modest profit.

He was happy when I came along and rented the apartment above his store because it had been vacant for almost a year. He had converted one of the bedrooms, originally part of the apartment I rented, into a storeroom. He thought it would be easier to rent a one bedroom. You could still see the outline of the old door Hewitt had patched when he moved the entrance into the hall outside. I wish I had the extra money to rent that other room. It would be perfect for my girls to stay overnight.

When he saw me, he stepped out onto the front walk.

"Good morning, Harry. Hey, you finished Billy's radio."

"Works like a charm," I said. "I'm sure he was missing it."

"Missing it," Hewitt said. "He's depressed without it."

"Well, it's the least I can do after what he sacrificed for all of us."

"Losing his leg was a tough break for him," Hewitt said.

I heard a tap from above and I saw Billy at his window. He could see that I was holding his radio and motioned that he was coming down.

"He looks anxious," Hewitt said.

"Sort of like being reunited with a loved one," I joked.

I could hear Billy coming down. His artificial leg gave him trouble on the stairs. When he opened the door, I saw him smile. That was the first time I had seen him smile. Probably the first time anyone in the neighborhood saw him smile.

"Hi, guys. Harry, it's fixed?" he asked.

"Good as before," I told him.

After the smile and hearing that it worked, I could almost see a tear come to his eye, but he quickly contained it. He couldn't hide how much it meant to him, though.

"Harry, would you stop up for a minute?" Billy asked.

"Sure, let me carry it up for you."

"That would be good," he said.

Hewitt had to get back to his store but I could see the surprised look on his face. Billy never invited anyone up to his apartment, let alone allowed anyone to help him carry anything for him. Billy told me to go up first and then followed me up. He refused to use a cane, pushing himself to do without one. Ben allowed him to have a banister installed on the opposite wall in addition to the original one. Having them on both sides helped him to climb the stairs. He told me the door was unlocked, so I opened it as he approached the top.

Billy's place was a single studio apartment, mostly bare of items, but neatly kept. There was a table and chair set up near a wire coming down from the ceiling. It was obvious that it was his radio table. Next to it, a couch, and opposite, a dresser and a bed, perfectly made in what I guessed was military style. His tiny kitchen area was just to the left inside the door and I could see a few cans of spaghetti in a row on the counter. I put the radio on the table and knelt down to plug it in. Billy came right over and began to attach the antenna. He turned on the power, dialed right to a channel and when he heard voices, he lit up and smiled again.

"You hear that," he said. "That's Duncan. He served in Afghanistan. Thanks again, Harry."

"I'm glad I could help, Billy."

"Since I got back it's been hard to get around, so that radio means a great deal to me. It's a way to keep in touch without the struggle. We got a great bunch of guys on there."

"I would like to hear about what happened in Iraq, if you're not uncomfortable talking about it," I said.

"Not with you, Harry. I was in the National Guard and working repairing trucks for Sal's trucks on 17M in Monroe. We were called up and deployed to Iraq. After being there for a few months we were on a mission to patrol the outer part of the city during the battle for Fallujah. I was with three of my best buddies when we were struck by a mortar shell. Two of them were killed, I lost my leg and our other buddy was in shock for some time. When he recovered I heard he was sent back. He's still there. All that time training, I had expected that things would have turned out differently."

"I'm sorry for all you lost," I told him.

I always believed that going into Iraq was a mistake. What a waste, I thought, of our brave soldiers who lost life and limb because of a trigger-happy president. What was worse, I thought, was how soldiers like Billy trusted they would be given the best equipment and training they could get. They were given the best of neither. Ben told me that they even tried to reduce Billy's benefits since he was wounded.

"Do you have family nearby?" I asked.

"I grew up in Monroe," he told me. "My mother died when I was young, but my Dad still lives there. It's too crowded there now and too pricey for me to afford. There's just my dad and me. I was told we have relatives on the West Coast, but I never met them."

I told him about Mom, a little about the girls and what had happened with Sarah. I never went into too much detail because nothing I had to complain about even came close to what Billy lived through.

"If you ever need a ride anywhere, just let me know," I told him.

Billy didn't have a car. There was a grocery store not too far to walk to, the deli below and most anything else he needed was here in the center of town.

"Thanks, Harry. There's a brass band playing next month in New Windsor, on Sunday July 2nd. One of my buddies on the air is in the band. Maybe we could go?" he asked.

Brass bands were not quite my cup of tea, but I told him we would.

"I saw you walking with Brice's daughter last night. She's looks like a sweet girl. How's that going?" he asked.

"Great," I said. "Lacie's one of the best things that ever happened to me."

"I like her dad," he said. "He treats everyone with respect. You can see that he really loves his daughter."

"He does everything for her," I said. "She's his life. I can really relate to him about that. I feel the same about my girls."

"I had a girlfriend when I shipped out for Iraq. But Nina left me shortly after I came back," he said. "She never said it was because I lost my leg but I knew, since she wrote me the whole time but left me when I got home. It must have been the reason, but I don't blame her though. Why would she want me now?"

I didn't know what to say, so I stayed silent. It was one tough break to find out the person you care about could just leave you like that. If you really love someone, it shouldn't matter. I thought about the thousands like Billy and what they must be going through. It just made me angrier about the senseless continuation of this failed war. Our President seemed only able to satisfy the corporations and had no problem funneling money to the rich.

I could understand why Billy never spoke out about anything though. He needed to feel that he lost his leg for the best of reasons. To me, it doesn't matter. Anyone's service is honorable. It's the civilian leaders I blame.

Billy is a nice guy when you get to know him. His tough exterior is just his way of keeping a bit of distance between most people and himself. I wasn't surprised at all that his apartment was so organized and uncluttered. It was how I pictured it. I saw Billy move to his radio a couple times and pull himself back to be polite. I had stayed a little long. It was obvious that he missed it and was getting anxious about getting to use it, so I told him that I had to get going.

"Billy, I'm sure you would like to tell your friends that you're back on the air," I said. "Remind me when it gets closer to the concert and we'll go. If you don't mind extra company, I'll invite Lacie to come with us."

"That would be great, Harry. Thanks again for everything."

As I walked down the stairs, I heard him tuning his radio dial. It really made me feel good that I could help him get back to his friends. I still had over an hour before I left for Mom's house and I saw Belita was in the deli, so I stopped in to thank her for the pie.

"Hi, Ben. Hi, Belita."

"Good morning, Harry," they said.

"Hewitt came in for change a little while ago and he told me you finished Billy's radio," Ben said.

"I did. He's upstairs talking with his friends already," I told them.

"I don't know what anyone would do without you around, Harry," Belita said. "You help everyone."

"I do what I can. I want to thank you for the pie, Belita."

"There will be more," she said. "It's the least I can do."

Belita asked about my mother and I told them about her being disoriented. I didn't need to go into too much detail. They just wanted me to know that they felt badly. Neither of them really knew her, but they expressed their best wishes for my mother. People around here had become sort of an extended family, ready to just listen when I needed it most.

"Pico told me you were with Lacie when he brought you the pie," Belita said.

Like any small community, word gets around fast.

"Really," Ben said.

"Yes. To tell you the truth, I really love her," I said.

"You two make a good couple," Belita said. "She's the sweetest girl in the neighborhood. I was happy to hear it."

"That's great," Ben said. "I can't imagine anyone who would be better for her. Have your girls gotten to meet her yet?"

"Not yet," I told them. "When things calm down we plan to take them out together."

"They'll really like her," Ben added.

"She makes it easier to deal with everything I am going through with Mom. I'm thrilled to have found her," I told them.

"And she's lucky to have found you too, Harry," Belita said.

"Thanks, you two."

"You know Harry, I asked if you would help Billy so I didn't want to trouble you further, but maybe sometime you could look at my clock?" Ben asked.

There was a large clock built into the wall over the tables and he told me it hadn't worked for a couple of years. I was surprised that I really hadn't paid attention to it before. I could see it was of good quality when it was bought. It had oversized arms and the metal lines for the hours were attached right on the wall surface. I took a quick look and saw there was a cover where the arms attached, held with only two screws.

"Do you have a small Philips screwdriver?" I asked.

He asked me to give him a moment as he pulled a small toolbox out from under the front counter and brought it over.

"You should have all you need in here," he said.

I found the correct screwdriver and removed the two screws from the cover plate. Careful of the arms, I pulled out the motor assembly and immediately saw a broken connection. It took only a moment to strip and reconnect it. Then I placed the motor back in and screwed on the cover. I looked at my watch and it showed ten twenty-five, so I set the arms to match. The clock only had the minute and hour hands, so I stood for a minute to watch the arm move.

"All set," I said.

They both just looked at me.

"What? It was a simple fix," I told them.

"I don't know where you get this stuff from," Ben said. "You fix every-thing."

"Not everything," I said.

"Well thanks, Harry. I always loved that clock. My father had it installed just before he died and he thought it was the greatest thing. I was almost ready to pull it off and patch the wall."

"You are something," Belita said.

"Well, thanks, you two."

We talked for a few more minutes and then I walked Belita outside. As an afterthought, Ben followed us out and handed me a large tub of vanilla ice cream.

"This will go good with the pie," he said.

"Thanks, Ben."

I told them I would see them later and went up to my place to put the ice cream away, but came right back down to leave. As I walked out of my bottom door, I saw two women across the street holding Bibles, knocking on the door of the first house past the stores. Two more were on my side and walked my way when they saw me. I remembered these folks from when Sarah and I lived outside of town.

They were like annoying sales people, the kind who never leave you alone to shop and follow you around trying to steer you toward a certain item. But the motive for these women is that they took it upon themselves to save the world by selling their moral view to everybody else. When they reached me, I could see their vacant look and forced smile.

"Good morning, sir," the short woman said. "Have you placed your trust in Jesus Christ?"

"Please. I'm not interested," I told her.

I really didn't need to hear this right now.

"God tells us through Romans 5:8, that even though Christ has died for us, we will not have his gift of eternal life until we decide to receive it."

I really hated when they quoted the Bible. They thought that, because it was written in a book they were told was the word of their God, then it was obviously true. They insisted they knew the only truth, while I believed them to be naive.

"Well, why would I want eternal life?" I asked. "How boring that would be. Besides, how do you know what your God would think? Because someone told you? I plan to live my life the best I can and then make way for my children, and hopefully grandchildren to have their time."

"It sounds like you hate God," the other woman said.

"I don't believe in your god. Why would I hate him?" I asked. "What I hate is being cornered by his sales people."

The vacant look was still present, but the smile had quickly gone away. I had no qualms about telling them how I felt. To me they were being intrusive.

"I feel sorry for you," the first woman added.

"Please don't," I said. "I could say the same of you both. You spend your time imposingly trying to sell your views to everyone. Because you think you're right, you believe that every other religion is wrong. Well, I simply believe that your religion is wrong as well."

The other woman opened her Bible and quickly turned to her book-marked page.

"It says here in Hebrews 11:6. But without faith it is impossible to please Him: for He that cometh to God must believe that He is, and that He is a rewarder of them that diligently seek him."

"Why would a god want anyone to please him?" I asked. "It sounds a bit human, don't you think? You give your God all the frailties of humans, jealousy, anger, things I hardly consider worthy of worship."

I could see they were becoming increasingly frustrated. Most people, although annoyed, would be polite, but I had no patience for them.

"Don't you fear death?" the first woman asked.

"No, I don't. It wouldn't matter anyway," I told them. "People are born, they live and then die. It's just a fact of life. It's a waste of time to worry about it."

"But don't you want to see your loved ones again in Heaven?" she asked.

"Just because you want something, doesn't mean it will happen," I said.

"We can see you won't listen to reason," the other added.

"What you profess is far from reason," I said. "To reason is to judge critically and I see none of that from people like you. Please, have a good life."

"May you one day find God," one of them said as they walked away.

The other told me to enjoy eternity in Hell. I got into my car and drove toward Mom's house.

Chapter 7

As I drove to Mom's house some scattered clouds moved in and it started to drizzle. I didn't want to listen to music on the way, so the wipers were louder than I was accustomed to. I hoped that Mom had a peaceful night and I wondered if there was a chance that her delusions would subside. I wanted so badly for the girls to be able to say goodbye to her. She was missing over two decades of her life, but at least she knew who I was. I found a little comfort in that. I thought again how things could always be worse. Mom taught me that. We could've had no time left at all. In the worst of times, she reminded me that somewhere, someone else had it far worse and that life goes on. Life would go on, but Mom wasn't coming with us this time.

It's funny how at the time Mom's lessons seemed quaint, but now as an adult I understood. Nonetheless, she knew that I had trouble containing my feelings when I read or heard about the worst of the worst. Stories of senseless tragedies troubled me too much. I empathized far too strongly, often dwelling on it for too long. When many turned to prayer, I knew it wasn't good enough. They wrote off tragedy much too easily because they believed that in death all things would be set right.

The rain was coming down steady and I realized I hadn't brought an umbrella. I didn't care much, though, since I had only a short distance to walk outside. When I parked in front I saw the rain pouring out of the broken downspout and I felt this old house was finally seeing its end as well.

Mom's parents left the house to her when they passed away before I was born and they always kept it repaired. My grandfather had a workshop in the basement and, although there were all the tools needed, my father hardly picked one up over the years. When I began to fix appliances and devices as a teenager, the shop made a great place for me to get away from the chaos going on upstairs.

My mother told me I inherited my knack for repairing things from her father. How he could fix anything. I wish that I had known her parents. It was hard to see the full dimension of someone from just a photograph and even less without color. I knew they were good people by the look on Mom's face when she spoke of them and the stories she remembered. Her memories of them were all good ones.

Mom told me she always saw her dad in me and I could tell from the few photographs she had. I saw it even more so as I got older. I couldn't help but think that, although Malcolm inherited his cleverness from Mom, he inherited his coldness of heart from our father. Evidently, Malcolm was able to live just fine with himself and his choices. I couldn't help but wonder what he told his son about Mom. Why if she was still alive, he had never met his grandmother. I wondered why his wife Julia never pushed him to at least invite the girls and me over for a visit, so at least the kids could meet.

I saw Maia in the window pulling one side of the curtain open, her face distorted by the sheets of rain rolling down the window glass. I wasn't sure if she could see me. The rain was steady, so I ran quickly to the porch and shook myself off. After a moment, I heard the dampened sound of Maia walking down the stairs so I knocked lightly. When she opened the door, I saw in her face that Mom was not doing so well today.

"Your mother is in the chair now, Harry, but she is beginning to drift off at times," Maia said.

"Thank you for caring for her," I said. "I know there won't be much we can do now, but everything you are doing is appreciated."

"She keeps asking for Malcolm," Maia said. "She says she wonders why he hasn't come home yet."

"I think I can calm her down about that," I told her. "I would get her lunch but if you wouldn't mind doing it, I would like to go right up."

"Of course, I'll bring it up soon," she said.

As I walked up the stairs, I heard my Mom talking, quieter at first, and clearer as I came closer to her room. She was talking about Malcolm with a sad voice. I opened the door and she was much more worn looking today, more slumped over. It was probably one of the saddest things

I would ever see or feel, to see Mom this way. I tried to look as positive as I was able to.

"Hi Mom," I said. "I just walked Malcolm to Daniel's. There was a short day at school. He said he hopes you're feeling better."

"You saw Malcolm," she said, finally calming a bit.

"Yes, Mom. I thought it wouldn't be the best thing for him to see you this sick."

"I was so worried about him. Thanks for looking after him."

"It's OK, Mom. You need to rest now and besides, Daniel's mother is fine with it."

I was happy I was able to convince her about Malcolm. Being her youngest, she always worried about him most. Even so, she continued to look a little anxious.

"I need to get better for Malcolm's graduation next week, she said. I just can't miss that. I know that next Monday they're bringing the kids to the middle school so they can see what it's like. I'm glad that you'll both be in the middle school together for at least the year. You can watch over him for a while."

"I will, Mom. You don't have to worry," I said.

It suddenly struck me why Mom had been having that pain in her leg. The week before Malcolm graduated from elementary school was when Mom tried to intervene as my father went to strike me. It was the time he pushed her down and she struck her leg on the table. She ended up in her bed for days and, when my father was working, Ruth came over to help her.

I remember that she was still limping the day that Malcolm graduated but was just well enough to go by then. Malcolm and I were embarrassed when people asked her how she hurt her leg, because we knew. She made up a convenient story about falling on the stairs. I remember how guilty I felt nodding in agreement. We never spoke about what went on in our house. Only a few people like Ruth knew about my father's temper and what really happened there.

At the time, I spoke to Mom very little about what happened that day. At twelve years old, I just avoided everything. I became anesthetized by the abuse and either hid or left the house when I could. I never thought about what Mom felt. Now I was seeing a side of the past I never had before. I could only imagine how alone she must have been. She had absolutely no one who could help her through the pain that my father inflicted on her, no one to say that things would be OK. Ruth was there to help Mom with groceries and making meals when she was ill, but she wasn't a very smart woman and contributed little to conversation. I remember that Mom would say that she had a heart of gold, though.

"Mom, I want you to think about getting better," I said. "I can take care of things until then."

"You are a good son, Harry. I appreciate that."

It was so hard now, with the hindsight of age, not to feel guilty about things I could have done. Things I never did. I felt worse when I remembered more about that time, as if I could have been any different at twelve years old.

I expected Maia would be bringing Mom's lunch soon, so I asked.

"Do you feel hungry, Mom?"

"Not too much, Harry."

"Well, Ruth was down in the kitchen when I came up and she was making lunch for you," I said.

"It's nice of her to do all these things for me," Mom said. "I will try to eat something if I can."

Mom was starting to drift off again. I could see her trying hard to stay focused because I was there, but at times she just couldn't. She would stare blankly and mutter a few words here or there. I just let her be for the time and then, after awhile, she looked up at me again. She was slumping further to one side so I went over to lift her up. I took an extra pillow from the bed and placed it on the arm of the chair for the side she was leaning to.

It was dark in the boy's room except for a small nightlight plugged into the socket on the wall. It was darker than usual with Malcolm's clothes piled against the wall, covering part of the light. But Harry could see that Malcolm's head was slipping off the bed, so he walked over, lifted him back onto his pillow and covered him with his blanket. He was relieved that the evening had gone by and his father hadn't come back. After taking a book from his dresser, Harry crawled into bed, pulled his blanket over him and turned on a small flashlight so he could read. He had barely gone through a few pages when he heard Malcolm turning in bed. He couldn't tell if he had woken but then heard Malcolm talk faintly to himself.

"Who's going to wash my cloths before I go back to school Monday?" *Malcolm almost whispered.*

Harry knew Malcolm was just speaking to himself, but answered him anyway.

"Don't worry, Malcolm. I will wash them for you. On Monday, I'll make sure you get up, and before I leave, I will get you ready for your bus. We can walk down the street so you can wait with Daniel if you like."

"OK. But I'm also supposed to bring three dollars for the party we're having in class," *Malcolm said.*

Harry reached over to his night table and pulled off the top of a tin can, where he kept his money. He took out three dollars and walked over to give it to his brother. Malcolm cupped the bills in his hands and held it under his blanket.

"Thanks, Harry," Malcolm said.

"We will work it out, Malcolm. I promise."

It was quiet in the room for a while, but Harry could hear his brother still turning in bed.

"Malcolm. Can't you sleep?" Harry asked.

"I'm trying to, but I keep waking up. I was thinking about something, Harry. Daniel's family believes in God. They say he watches over people. Do you think it's true?"

"Not over us, Malcolm."

Mom took care of us for so long, but I never pictured she would need me to care for her like this. I heard Maia coming up the stairs and I walked out of the room for a moment.

"Thanks, Maia," I said. "Mom is drifting off again. Please, let me take that. I'm sure she'll wake up soon."

I took the tray and placed it on the table next to Mom's chair. I waited patiently for Mom to be responsive, but I almost dosed off when I heard her again.

"Harry, I must have fallen asleep," she said.

"Ruth didn't want to disturb you, but she brought up your lunch."

"I will try to eat something then," she said.

Everything she did took great effort for her now. As she ate, it reminded me of a wounded animal desperately trying to eat for the energy to heal. Again, she held the half of a sandwich in both hands taking little bites and concentrating on the next. It seemed more of an exercise in survival than an enjoyable meal. She nibbled around the edges and left most of both halves on the plate.

She looked at the tray for a moment and asked, "Would you ask Ruth if she could make me a cup of coffee?"

She stopped drinking coffee when my father passed away, since most times it was he who insisted on her making some all the time. Growing up there was always a pot on.

"I'll go down and get one for you," I said.

I knew there would still be coffee in the kitchen. She always kept some for when I came by and the nurses had brought some of their own. I walked down and stopped in the sitting room where Maia was.

"Mom is asking for some coffee," I told her.

"She asked for some at breakfast this morning as well," Maia said.

I explained how she had given it up years ago and it was strange to hear her ask for a cup. I told Maia that I would make it and asked her if she would like some, which she did. She said she took it black with no sugar. Mom still had the coffee pot that belonged to her mother and I'm sure the nurses were having a bit of a hard time figuring it out. Her coffee pot was an old steel colored percolator with the glass bulb on the cover and metal insert with a coffee strainer at the top. The water would boil through the tube and you could see through the glass bulb when it looked dark enough. Many of the kitchen items were left from when my grandparents passed away. Mom said they gave her good memories.

A few of the old appliances still worked as well because, when I started to fix things as a teenager, they were my first repairs. I remembered each appliance and what had gone wrong. This house was just packed with memories, good and bad. While I waited, I looked out the back window into the yard. The old shed had collapsed from age, but was still left there in a pile. That shed was where Malcolm and I put on little plays for the neighborhood kids. We wrote a short script, practiced, and then charged the kids a nickel to come watch our performance.

Just to the right of the old shed was the gate on the back fence. It led into the woods that went on for acres. The woods were owned by the county and never sold because much of it was wetlands. Memories were coming back to me so strong now. When Mom passed, the house would be sold and all this would be gone for me. Even with my father being so imposing, I always thought of it as Mom's house and I hated to see it falling apart.

When the coffee looked ready I poured it, placed the mugs on a small tray and stopped to give a cup to Maia in the sitting room.

"Here you are, Maia. Be careful. That coffee pot makes it very hot."

"Thanks. I had trouble with that thing, but I think I'm finally getting the hang of it," she said.

"I can understand that," I told her. "I think the only place that still has one like that is the Smithsonian. It always reminded Mom of her mother and those were her best memories."

"With your Mom so sick, it's hard to really get to know her, but she seems like a nice woman," Maia said.

"She always had a kind heart and meant well. My father was abusive to her but he never changed that in her."

"Why doesn't your brother come see her?" she asked.

"He never understood that Mom was also a victim. He blames her for what our father did to us."

"It's sad," she said. "You would think, in hindsight, he would reconsider his feelings."

"You would think," I said.

"What did he say when you told him your Mom was dying?" she asked.

"I haven't talked to him in years. I hadn't planned on telling him."

"Maybe you should. Maybe he has second thoughts. You should leave that decision to him, whether to come or not."

I told her I would think about it.

The coffee cooled enough so I went back upstairs to Mom's room. I heard her talking to herself again, but this time with a calmer tone. When I opened the door, I saw Mom had slumped over again so I placed the tray down on the dresser and helped her to sit up.

"Thank you, Harry," she said.

"Oh, that's OK Mom. I'm glad to spend some time with you, and help."

I removed the lunch tray and put the coffee on the small table. When Mom took the first sip, I could tell that it was finally something she enjoyed.

"You did a good job making this," she said. "Since when are you drinking coffee?"

I was sipping my mug, but had forgotten that I never drank coffee when I was twelve. It must have looked a bit unusual.

"Oh, I just thought I would have some this time with you. It's OK," I told her.

"I'm so sorry for what your dad did to you the other day," she said.

"He is only my father," I told her. "You are my mother and my Mom. He has never been a dad."

"I wish I had an excuse or an explanation for you, Harry. I really do. If only I had the courage to throw him out for what he does to you kids. I'm afraid of what it may be like if I did, but I'm also afraid of what he's doing to you two as well," she told me.

"We'll be alright, Mom. I just want you to feel better."

"I do, Harry. It makes me feel better to talk with you. You are becoming a responsible young man, and I can't tell you what a relief it is just having you around right now."

I felt guilty that back then, I wasn't. I could still feel relieved that, at least it was what she needed now, and I was here this time. Inside I wanted to tell her how the girls were doing, that I had fallen in love with Lacie and all the other things now going on in my life, but this would have to do.

Again she drifted off and I walked over to look out the window. The rain had stopped and the sun was beginning to peek out, so I opened the curtains to let in a little light. The room was a bit stuffy and I cracked the window a few inches, and felt a slight breeze coming in. For a moment there was the smell of dust from the aging screen.

Outside the window was the roof of the front porch and it made me think of the time Malcolm and I came home to find the door locked. Mom just walked up to the corner store but we didn't know. Malcolm gave me a boost so I could climb up the drainpipe and enter the window to get in. The little tear I made to slip my finger in was still on the screen.

I went over to the shelf and examined all the little things Mom saved over the years. They were of no real interest to me growing up. They were little statues and dolls, some from her mom and other items like the art projects we made for her when we were in elementary school. Until I got older, I never understood why she cherished them so much. Everything was dusty, so I took a rag from the closet outside her door and started to carefully dust them off. It took some time to do them all, but when I was just about finished, I heard Mom stirring again.

"What are you doing, Harry?" she asked.

"I just thought I would dust off some of your things, Mom."

"How thoughtful," she said. "You don't have to do that. I will be better soon and I can do it then."

"It's no trouble. I was enjoying looking at these things we made for you."

"Those are my favorite possessions," she said.

The last item I dusted was a clay ashtray that I made for her. No one who ever came over used it and she would never have let anyone anyway. I put down the rag and went back to sit with Mom.

"Harry, I know that I'm not well, but I need to see Malcolm. Can you please make sure he doesn't stay at Daniel's house tomorrow? And if you see them playing nearby today, ask him to just come in for a moment."

I didn't know what to say, but it was easiest to just say yes, knowing I would have to keep coming up with stories. Again it got me angry that I had to lie because of Malcolm just walking away from us. All of this energy spent feeling this way when he, with no conscience, felt nothing, I'd bet.

"I am so sorry that you both had to put up with your father the other day."

"It's all him, Mom. What do you possibly have to feel sorry for? He's just a bastard," I said.

"Harry, your language," she said.

"I'm sorry, Mom, but you know it's true."

"I know," she said. "But what would you have me do, Harry?"

"I want you to do what makes you happy," I said. "But stop blaming yourself."

That time was long gone and it made little sense to regret the past. I hated that she beat herself up over my father's actions. I just wanted her to feel comfortable.

We sat together and talked, but Mom would slip off more and more as the afternoon went on. In a coherent moment, I told her that I was going to leave and do some things. I kissed her on her forehead and turned to walk out.

"Harry, please don't forget to have Malcolm stop up for a moment if you see him."

"I won't forget, Mom," I said. "I will see you later."

She seemed so much worse today that I wondered if there would be a later. I walked back to her chair and hugged her and kissed her head again.

"Goodbye, Mom. I love you."

"I love you too, Harry."

I hesitated for a brief moment and then left.

Maia heard me coming down the stairs and came out of the sitting room.

"How is she now?" she asked.

"She looks much worse today. I know that Ms. Barnes is coming soon to relieve you. Can you please ask her to call me if there is any change?" I asked.

"I will," Maia said.

"She can call me any time at all. I will have my cell phone."

"Grace will be coming to stay overnight and I will make sure Ms. Barnes tells her as well. I will be here in the morning, of course."

"Thank you," I said.

Mom was really struggling with the past. I only hoped that when her time came, she would feel at peace.

I went down the front steps to the walk and, as I turned, I noticed something peculiar about Mom's window. The glass looked strangely opaque. Even more unusual was that her window frame looked newer, cleaner, than the others. She did pay Eddie, from two houses over, for help around the house. But I couldn't see why someone would bother to maintain just the one window. Mom was in no condition to hire Eddie now, so I wondered why I hadn't noticed it before.

Chapter 8

I was in my car driving home and I couldn't help but feel that Maia had a point about leaving the decision up to Malcolm. Why should I feel guilty for the rest of my life by not giving him the choice to make amends if he wanted to? It was best to clear my conscience. I would reach out one last time to my brother. Mom really wanted to see him, so I resigned myself to doing my best to convince him to come visit her. If I called, he could likely just blow me off, so I decided to drive to his home.

His high school friend, Jeff, still kept in touch with him, so when I got to town, I turned left on route 94 toward Chester. Jeff lived just a short drive away on Hudson Road. I would just stop by and see if he was home. He would understand my not calling before stopping by. When I was close to his house, I saw him getting into his car. I pulled up and lowered my window.

"Jeff, I'm sorry to just stop by, but I have something important to ask you. Let me pull my car over."

He nodded that he would wait, so I parked and walked over.

"Jeff, I'm sure you didn't know but my mother is dying and I don't think she has more than a day or two. I need you to give me Malcolm's address. He should know."

"I understand Harry. He moved to Sparta, in New Jersey. Mohawk Avenue. It's about an hour and a half drive."

I asked him to give me a moment and I went over to get a pen from my car. As he told me, I scribbled the address and phone number on the back of a crinkled business card I had in my wallet.

"Thanks Jeff, I really appreciate it. I'm sorry if I held you up."

"That's OK Harry. It's no trouble. I feel bad about your mother."

I gestured goodbye and got back into my car. I waited for Jeff to pull away first and then I drove back into town. Although I had the phone number, I'd already decided I wouldn't call. Not even to let Malcolm know I was coming. When I got back to my apartment, I turned on my laptop and used Mapquest to print out the directions. I had been to Sparta one time before. There was a cozy lake community called Lake Mohawk that was the kind of neighborhood I pictured Malcolm would move to. I didn't want to go alone unless I had to, so I thought I'd call Lacie and see if she would take the ride with me. She had finished work by now, so I pressed in the phone number.

When it rang more than six times I was feeling disappointed, but then she answered.

"Hello."

"Hi, Lacie. It's me, Harry."

"Hi, Harry. How was your mother today?" she asked.

"She's doing badly, Lace. I don't really know if she'll last another day."

"I'm so sorry. Would you like me to come by again?" she asked.

"Well actually, I was going to ask if you would take a ride with me. I need to go to New Jersey. Mom keeps asking for Malcolm and I'm going to try and convince him to come see her."

"I'm glad you decided to tell him Harry. As long as he knows, you can feel assured that you did everything you could."

"I'd like to come right over and pick you up. As much as I would love to see your place, it will have to be another time. I'm just going to tap the horn, so we could leave right away."

"I'll be waiting," she said.

Lacie gave me her address and I left right away. When I went down to my car, I quickly scooped up the spent juice bags and wrappers that the girls left, as well as trash that missed the bag which I hung on the ashtray draw I used for coins. I put the directions printout on the visor and left for Lacie's house. I was relieved that I wouldn't be going alone because, although I had resigned myself to visiting Malcolm, I still felt unnerved by the sick feeling it gave me in my stomach.

In some ways I missed my little brother, but at the same time I was mad as hell at him for his callous treatment of Mom and me, but most especially of Mom. I rehearsed in my head some of the things I would say, knowing full well that things never go as planned. I never even met Julia and Brian but always wondered about them. I knew it wasn't the best way to meet them, but what choice did I have? I always went along with Malcolm's insistence on isolating himself and his family from us, but if there was ever a good reason to contact him, it was now.

I was getting close, so I looked carefully for Lacie's street. It was right off Route 94, not much further than where Jeff lived. Then I saw it just up ahead. It was a street lined with trees that had grown so tall they lifted the sidewalks near their roots. It's a nice neighborhood, I thought, with kids playing in the street. It reminded me of my street when I was growing up. I was looking for number twenty eight, but then I saw Lacie sitting on her front steps, waiting.

She was sitting with a little girl and was fixing her little friend's shirt collar. Lacie looked so beautiful in a soft spring dress, pastel blue with red stitching at the bottom and on the shortened sleeves. She had a small night bag at her side. Every time I saw her, I fell even more in love with her. As Lacie walked to the car, the little girl ran to a friend on the sidewalk. Both were looking to catch a glimpse of who I was.

"Hi, Harry," Lacie said. "The girls wanted to see who I had been talking about."

"Hi girls," I said through the open car door.

They waved and giggled as they talked to each other. Lacie threw her bag in the back, closed the door and we left.

"Thanks for coming with me, Lacie."

"I told you Harry. I want to be here for you," she said.

"Well, it helps a great deal," I told her. "I know it's not the best way to start a relationship."

"What we want can wait," she said. "This is far more important now."

I told Lacie stories about Malcolm, about when we were kids and more about our house. There were good moments, but fewer than the bad. I explained how, when our father was abusive, we would go off together to hide and help each other cope. I told her about the closet in Mom's room. When we were older, Malcolm started staying with friends and we drifted in opposite directions. But I knew it was our father who had ripped our family apart, slowly over time. I told her how, right up to his death, my father never admitted to ever doing anything wrong.

It was always someone else's fault when he was abusive. Once I had grown, I only despised my father. He thought nothing about Malcolm taking off after finishing school. Just as he thought nothing about, how once I moved, I only met up with Mom when he wasn't around. He simply branded us ungrateful.

I asked Lacie about her life as a child and she told me how, after her Mom died, she could remember most everything since. She said that, for more than a year, she was angry that her mom was taken from her, but then realized it did her no good to feel that way. Her father told her after she had grown up, how it crushed him, but he hid that from her so well at the time. He would trust a friend to watch the tavern so he could be there for every school function. It was obvious she was the center of his life.

Lacie felt that her Dad was driven to provide her with all the attention anyone else would get with both parents. She told me that when they moved to Washingtonville it was just a little more than two years after her mother died. They immediately felt at home there. When they first came into New York City, at the advice of a new acquaintance, they visited upstate and fell in love with the area. It fulfilled the dream his wife and he had to open a small business in America, after they scrimped and saved for so long.

The tavern became his place of comfort and anyone who entered his door was to be given respect. In turn, it earned him the respect of his customers. She told me how enjoyable it was growing up at the tavern because she ended up with the largest family of all. All the regulars watched as she grew from a child into a young woman.

We had just passed the border into New Jersey and I was starting to feel that sense of fight or flight, uncontrollable at times to us all. It was a bit obvious and Lacie could see it in my face.

"It will be alright, Harry, you're doing the right thing," she said.

"I guess, Lacie. It just feels strange, and I have no idea what will happen."

"Well, in an hour or so, you'll no longer have that feeling," she said.

What an interesting observation, I thought. It would be over soon, one way or the other.

We talked a while longer and as we drove I noticed we were getting close to Sparta. We passed a lake and were coming up on Mohawk Avenue where Malcolm lives. The town is nice, with neatly kept yards and freshly cut lawns. I drove up Mohawk and found the address I was given by Jeff. When we parked, I saw it was a nice home, brick, with a two-car garage and well-lit front entrance.

"Well, we came all this way so we might as well go in," I said attempting a little levity.

I could see a shadow on the curtain in the front window, so I knew someone was home. When we got out of the car to walk up the sidewalk, Lacie took my hand. I gave her a brief kiss and we went up to ring the doorbell. Through the curtained glass on the door we could see the silhouette of someone coming to answer it. The door opened and we saw a woman with a small boy behind her legs. I knew it must be Julia and Brian.

"Hello, can I help you?" she asked.

Julia was thin, with a pleasant look on a warm face. Brian looked just like Malcolm did at his age.

"You must be Julia and that must be Brian," I said. "I'm Harry Ladd."

"Mommy, he has our name," Brian said, coming out from behind his Mom.

"I'm your dad's brother, Brian. I'm your uncle Harry. This is Lacie." I added.

"Please, come in," Julia said.

Julia looked a bit conflicted. She seemed interested in meeting me, but must have been concerned about what Malcolm would think. Julia knew that Malcolm had a brother back in New York, but she also knew that he wanted little to do with me. I introduced Lacie to Julia and explained briefly about my girls and how they lived with their mother. I told Brian a little about Kaela and Lainey and how I wished he could meet his cousins. I could see that it was all foreign to him. Malcolm evidently never mentioned us to Brian.

"Malcolm should be home soon," Julia said. "He was working late, but called a short while ago to let me know he was leaving the office. It's not more than thirty minutes from here. Come, let me show you into the den. You can wait for him in there."

"Thanks, Julia," I said. "I would not have barged in like this if it were not so important. I know Malcolm has his issues with our mom, but she's dying, Julia, and she is asking for him. I thought it would be best to tell him in person."

"I understand," she said. "I'm sorry to hear that she's ill."

She opened the two sliding doors and showed us in.

Brian came over to his mother and asked, "Who's dying Mom?"

"She's your Grandmother. It's your father's mother," she told him. "You never met her."

Brian was satisfied with that answer and went over to play with some toys. The den had a small fireplace nestled between built-in shelves full of books, a couch and loveseat at a right angle with a small coffee table. It looked just like a den would look, complete with a magazine rack and double wooden sliding doors. I noticed a crucifix and a silver plaque hanging on the back wall, with the "Lord's Prayer" engraved on it. Malcolm never had religion in his life, so I assumed that they were Julia's.

Lacie sat down on the couch next to Julia and began to talk with her, so I took a moment to go over and speak with Brian. He looked so much like Malcolm and I could see he was growing up happy. Even by Brian's age, Malcolm had already been riddled with abuse by our father. I could almost see why Malcolm wanted to shield his family from his past, but he never had to take it as far as he did.

"So Brian, how is school this year?" I asked.

"Great," he said. "My teacher is nice."

"I'm glad. You know, you look a lot like your Dad," I said.

He just looked at me and smiled. I told him how his cousin Lainey was just about his age and that Kaela was two years older. Brian was the only cousin Kaela and Lainey had.

"You would love your cousins, Brian," I told him.

He asked me why they don't come over and I told him I didn't know. One day I hoped they would all get to meet each other.

"Your dad never told you about us?" I asked.

"I don't remember," Brian said.

"Brian, I'm happy I got to meet you now."

We heard a car door close just outside and Julia thought it must be Malcolm, so she got up to greet him at the door.

She called to Brian, "Come on honey, let's give your dad some privacy to talk with your uncle alone."

She looked at me for a moment.

"I will tell Malcolm you're here and send him in," Julia said.

"Thank you, Julia, it was so nice to finally meet you and Brian," I told her.

"I'm glad as well," she said. "It was nice to meet you also, Lacie."

Julia is a pleasant woman and I could easily see why Malcolm married her. It seemed that she had just been doing what Malcolm wanted. As we waited, we heard the front door open and Julia talking briefly with Malcolm. When he walked through the doorway he had a puzzled look on his face. He stepped in and Julia pulled the doors closed from outside the room. Malcolm looked a bit older, but he was able to remain thin. He had that business-like part in his hair, but the part combed over, didn't quite make it to the other side.

"Hi Malcolm, you look well," I said. "This is Lacie."

"Harry, what are you doing here?" he asked with a look of disgust.

I could see he was beginning to turn red.

"Really, Malcolm, we haven't talked in years and that's how you put it? OK, Malcolm. Mom's dying and could be gone at any moment. She wants to see you and I thought you might want to know. I didn't want her to die without giving you a chance to say goodbye."

"Well, I'm sorry you wasted a trip, Harry."

I was completely stunned by Malcolm's cold response, when all I wanted to do was let him know his mother was dying.

"Damn you, Malcolm, you're thirty-four years old. It's about time you grew up. You can't drag this crap around your whole life. You need to get over it already."

"Don't lecture me, Harry. I'm the one with the solid family while Jeff told me you split up with your wife. And here you are with a girlfriend. I even take my family to church." he said.

Lacie sunk into the couch and didn't say a word.

Even take my family to church, I thought. He shuns his mother, and then professes how holy he is the very next moment. Something is seriously wrong here.

"And that makes it OK?" I asked. "What a hypocrite. You refuse to see your mother and then brag to me about how you go to church. Please spare me your sanctimonious bullshit, Malcolm."

"What would you know about it, Harry? You've always been an atheist. What kind of example are you setting for your kids? And now they're growing up in a broken family."

"Sarah left me, Malcolm. I had no choice. Not that it's any of your business anyway."

"Well, maybe if you had learned to follow the teachings of the church, you would've stayed together."

I could see why Malcolm might join a church. Maybe he felt it was right for him, Julia and Brian. But never would I have expected that he would use it to attack me, or to justify what he did to Mom.

"Are you insane in there? Where did my brother's mind go? I came here to tell you that your mother is dying and all you can do is point out my misfortunes. Answer this Malcolm: How Christian is it to deny your dying mother a visit or to hurt her all these years? She loves you, Malcolm. Don't you understand that?"

"I have no mother and I don't want you corrupting my family either."

"Malcolm, what harm would it do to visit her?" Lacie asked. "Harry didn't tell you but your mother is having delusions. She thinks you're ten years old and she sees Harry as twelve. It's causing her great pain worrying about you."

"Really, and what do you have to do with this?" Malcolm asked.

"I love your brother," Lacie said. "I care about your Mom and what Harry is going through."

"Well, you don't understand."

"She does understand, Malcolm. She understands compassion for a woman who cares about you. Mom was a victim. There was nothing she could do about our father. Do you remember the week before you left elementary school when he hurt Mom so badly that she could hardly walk? She's living it again. She has advanced brain cancer and it's causing delusions. The only thing she's been thinking about is whether you're OK. It's been giving me insights into how sorry she felt for us then. Things we never knew."

"Good for you, Harry. I have no interest in going."

"How can you say that, Malcolm? What could possibly make you do this to Mom?"

"You both brought your problems on yourselves," he said. "You deny the Lord, and Mother had little time for him while we were growing up."

"There are always bad things that happen in life. Nobody is to blame for it. You just choose to ignore it all," I said.

"Well, tell me, Harry, who has the better family? Me with mine or you with what's left of yours?" he asked.

"I can see you are doing well, Malcolm, but you can't just ignore us and hope your past will go away. How we deal with the bad things in life defines us as much as how we deal with the good," I said.

"Julia and I put our faith in the Lord and he takes care of the bad."

"No, Malcolm, you ignore the bad. Your Lord is taking care of nothing. You're sticking your head in the sand, blocking your ears."

"You are no example for me, big brother," he said. "What have you accomplished?"

"I've accomplished many things. But you evidently wouldn't view them as having value."

"Then they have no value," he said.

"I can see I'm getting nowhere with you. I shouldn't have come. "Come on Lace, let's go home."

"I didn't ask you to come, Harry," he said.

I didn't say another word to him as we let ourselves out. He didn't even get up to watch us leave. He just sat there. When we were getting into the car, I could see Julia looking out from the upstairs window. I looked at her for a moment, trying to see how she felt. But saw nothing.

I could not have felt a deeper despair as we got into my car to drive home.

"Lacie, could it have worked out any worse?" I asked.

"I know how much this must hurt you, Harry. I'm sorry your brother disappointed you."

"I just can't understand it," I said. "How could he have changed so much?"

I couldn't help but run the scene back through my mind, trying to think of what I might have said differently that could have made Malcolm change his mind. A useless exercise until I realized there was nothing I could have said. I felt it would be the last time I saw him. As much as I felt angry at Malcolm, I still missed the way my brother used to be. I didn't want to lose my little brother.

When we were close to home, Lacie asked me not to drop her off.

"I want to stay again, Harry. I brought clothes in my bag. Would that be OK?"

It was more than OK. I needed her to stay.

"I would like nothing more, Lace."

It made it so much easier with Lacie staying with me. With so much hurt, she gave me something beautiful to think about. When we went to bed, we just held each other. I was looking in her eyes.

"Lacie, I love you," I said.

"I love you too, Harry. Don't let what your brother said hurt you."

She kissed me on my forehead and I fell asleep.

Chapter 9

For a moment when I woke, I thought I had just fallen asleep but when I turned, I saw that Lacie had already gone. She must have awakened before the alarm and shut it off. There was a note:

> "I didn't want to trouble you with everything going on.
> My co-worker Beth comes in from Cornwall and she's
> going to take me to my car on her way to work.
> I left my bag on the night table. I can get it later.
> I love you,
> Lacie"

With everything going on, it was great to have Lacie's support. Even in the best of times, Sarah never made me feel that I was all that special to her, but with Lacie it was effortless.

It was barely eight in the morning, but I knew I couldn't sleep any longer. I put on my robe and went into the kitchen to make some coffee. I made it a little stronger than usual and it smelled great as it brewed. I stood there for a moment taking it in like a drug. When it was ready, I poured a cup and went to sit by the window. I looked out and saw a string of cars heading toward Salisbury Mills. They were most likely commuters to Manhattan on their way to the train parking lot. They were always the ones who slowed down as they passed the police station up the road.

It was sunny and beautiful outside, the opposite of what I was feeling inside. Malcolm disappointed me. I found it strange that he could deny his dying mother's wish to see him, while believing himself to be virtuous. I wouldn't have guessed that Malcolm would turn out this way, but so much about people who profess what he did, baffled me. They complicate their lives with rituals, pretending that we're more than human, masking the reality of how fragile, how breakable we all are.

They think they'll find their answers in a book and insist that only through their God can we attain eternal life. How so, when so many people in this world are barely able to just stay alive and have no hope of ever learning about their savior? Was the intense suffering of those millions provided merely to test the faithful? What a thoughtless god it would be to devise such a cruel trick. To me it's absurd.

I promised Mom I'd make sure that Malcolm came home, so what would I tell her now? I was able to stifle her worries so far but it was getting increasingly more difficult. I finished my coffee and grabbed some clothes to go shave and shower. These were the times I hated standing in front of the mirror, when it forced me to see expressions I couldn't help but make. I stepped into the shower and felt the warm water hitting my skin. I could smell the soap rising in the steam and it felt relaxing for the moment. Even after I washed, I just stood there letting the water hit me. Then I heard the phone ringing. The water had been washing over my ears so I wasn't quite sure how many times it had rung already. I got out as quickly as I could, wrapping a towel around me but still dripping into the living room.

"Hello?"

"Hello, Harry, it's Maia. Your Mom is not doing well this morning. She couldn't even get up to sit in the chair today and her breathing is much shallower. You might want to come here sooner."

"I will, Maia. I'll get dressed and be right there. Thanks for calling me."

I rushed into my clothes and with my hair still wet, quickly grabbed my things and left. There were still the morning commuters to contend with and the traffic light at Route 208 seemed to stay red for a lifetime. How incredibly slow the world around you moves when you need to be somewhere. There was no choice but to join the long line of commuters and hope that I could get there soon enough. The few lights there were turned red several times as the line backed up from the cars turning onto Route 17.

When I finally got there and parked, I looked up at Mom's window and the glass looked opaque again. This time, not only did her window frame look newer and cleaner than the others, the siding was clean in a circle, all around the frame. Who the hell was maintaining the house with all this going on? And right outside Mom's room. Maia heard me walking on the porch and came out.

"Hello, Harry," she said. "Your mother had almost nothing to eat this morning. I tried for some time to get her to eat more but she couldn't."

"Thanks, Maia. I'll see what I can do. Maia have you seen anyone working on the house in the last few days?"

"Not while I was here. Nobody. What do you mean?" she asked.

"Never mind, Maia, we can talk about it later. I'm going to go right up."

"I left a couple cups of pudding on the table," she said. "Maybe you could get her to eat a little. She's very sick now, Harry."

"Thanks, Maia," I said. "I really appreciate all you're doing."

"It's no trouble," she said. "I want you to know that your mother kept asking for your brother again. I told her that he might be with you. I just didn't know what to say."

"I went to his home last night. Malcolm won't be coming, Maia."

"He knows how ill she is and he still wouldn't come?" she asked.

"He's angry with Mom," I said. "He's also angry with me, for some twisted reason."

I started toward the stairs as Maia continued.

"You would think that a son could forgive his mother, in light of what she's going through," she said.

"You would think so," I told her.

"Family is what you need most in times like these. If I can get anything for you, just let me know," she said.

"Thanks Maia."

As I walked up the stairs I heard nothing, no sound. It seemed as I got closer to the room, that even the sounds from the reverberations of my footsteps on the wall were diminishing. Maia left the door open so, when I was close, I could see Mom lying in bed with the pillows propping up her head and back. Her head was turned away. I was feeling profoundly sad, so I stopped for a moment to compose myself. I needed for her to feel comforted by my visit, not to worry because this was hurting me. I hoped she wouldn't ask about Malcolm because I didn't have time to think of a believable excuse.

Something felt stranger today, beyond the sadness of losing Mom. I wiped the last small tear from my chin and thought I'd better not wait any longer.

When I entered the room, I felt a vibration run through me. I was stung with a bright light that felt as if it burst behind my eyes. It took a moment to adjust, but when I could see again, I saw objects in the room changing. I felt sick to my stomach. On Mom's night table I saw her new lamp begin to fade and disappear while a hammer appeared in the center of her night table. The room was surrounded by light and sounds were still. I heard nothing.

I remembered that hammer because it belonged to my Grandfather, but I didn't want to admit it to myself. The head had snapped off and it had been thrown away long ago. But it was there on the table, just the way it was in the past. The time Mom believed she was living in. I could never forget. I remembered how I watched her hang that photo on the wall and then place that hammer there. It remained on her table for days until she was able to walk again.

I turned back, and in the mirror over the dresser opposite Mom's bed, I saw a twelve-year old boy.

Me.

Something absolutely amazing was happening. I couldn't imagine how but I entered the delusions Mom had been trapped in for the last several days. Of all the things in the Cosmos and on earth, I couldn't think how. It was extraordinary. No one would ever believe me. As intriguing as it was, I was frightened and wanted to leave. But then I heard Mom.

"Who's there?"

Mom's voice sounded distressed and she tried to turn but couldn't.

"Mom, it's me, Harry."

I went around and sat on the side of the bed so she could look at me without turning. Mom looked gravely ill, but her face appeared decades younger, as it did back then. I was panic stricken, but I couldn't leave her now.

"Where's Malcolm?" she asked struggling to speak.

"He'll be home later, Mom."

I just couldn't think of anything else to say.

"I want to talk with you both," she said.

"I'm here, Mom, and Malcolm will be here later."

She hesitated for a time as she attempted to reach out her hand. I moved closer and held her arm.

"Harry, are you happy?" she asked.

"I'm happy enough, Mom," I told her. Life is what it is. It's up to me to make the best of it."

If Mom was not as ill, she might have realized that at twelve, I wouldn't have thought or talked that way. I wasn't sure of anything then. But it was how I felt now.

"You've helped me a great deal in the last few days, Harry. I want to thank you for that. You're really growing into a fine young man."

"Thanks Mom. I'm trying the best I know how."

I couldn't help but think about how my marriage ended, how I never was able to get enough time with my daughters and how I still hadn't finished my studies. So many things just didn't quite go my way, but it was true that I was trying my best. Maybe it was good that she didn't remember what was to come for her family.

"Do you think Malcolm is happy?" Mom asked.

"I don't know Mom. I guess, enough."

It annoyed me for a moment, and it was one of those times when I couldn't help my expression. I worried that she would see how disappointed I felt about Malcolm. At least it wouldn't break her heart, knowing how he feels about her now. To me he was being cowardly.

"You're able to keep what your father does from affecting you, Harry, but it's not the same for Malcolm," she said. "I see he's frightened."

"You need to stop dwelling on this Mom. You need to concentrate on getting better."

I wanted her to stop worrying.

"But I need to talk about it, Harry. I need you to understand that it's never my intention to let anything hurt you two."

"I know that, Mom. You're as much a victim as we are. You know there's nothing you can do to change him."

"But what about me?" she asked. "Can you forgive me for not stopping him? Can you forgive me for being afraid?"

"He frightens all of us, Mom. Only he's to blame and it makes me angry to see how he treats you. You know what he did when you tried to stop him from hitting me."

"My leg will heal, Harry. But will my family?"

I was seeing a side of Mom I never saw through twelve-year-old eyes. I regretted the times I ran away from my problems, never caring what Mom was going through. If only I had been there for her. Maybe back then she only needed someone to talk to, someone to listen. It seemed that, as much as I wanted her to forget, she needed to get things off her chest.

"It makes me sad that he makes you to feel this way, Mom. You have a kind heart and I despise him for what he's done to you. I hate him for what this does to us all."

He had the ability to inflict pain even up to Mom's last hours. So much of her life was consumed by wasted energy for a man who did nothing but abuse her.

"I realize that now, Harry. I'm glad that you're honest with me. I didn't want to see before. You never really told me how much this affected you."

"I'm sorry, Mom. You really don't need to hear this right now."

"I do need to hear it," she said. "I wanted to ask you but I hadn't the courage until now. I was ignoring things, hoping it would change. I realize now that he will never change."

I still felt unnerved about what was happening in my mind, but Mom needed me here. If it made her feel better to talk about it, I would listen, as painful as I saw the memories were for her. She struggled again to turn her head and sit up, but couldn't.

"I'm tired, Harry," she said. "I wish I could get up and sit with you but I'm just so tired."

"Would you like to sleep for awhile?" I asked.

"No, Harry. Please don't leave me. I don't want to sleep yet," she said.

"OK, Mom, don't worry, I won't leave."

"I wish Malcolm were here. Will he be home soon?" she asked.

"I'm just not sure," I told her. "He's studying for a test with Daniel and I told him it would be alright with you."

"The way he looked the other day, I could see he was hurting," she said. "He's just a little boy and it tortures me to see how affected he is by this, how you both are. When he comes home, I want to tell him how sorry I am for what your father is putting you both through."

"When I see him, I'll ask him to come up and talk with you," I told her.

I wondered how long excuses about Malcolm would work before Mom finally realized something was wrong. She looked so helpless to me, not only from her illness, but also because of how relentlessly the past was haunting her. I questioned what was worse: to know you're dying or to be trapped in one of the most difficult times of your life. All I wanted to do was to make her feel better, but it seemed I might have caused her even more guilt. I wasn't the twelve-year-old she saw me as. I knew everything to come and it was difficult playing the boy who didn't care. I just wasn't any good at it.

"Harry, I don't want to feel this way anymore. Talking to you made me realize what's important and nothing is more precious to me than you two. I love you, Harry."

"I love you, too, Mom."

I watched tears begin to roll over her nose and onto the bed. She struggled to straighten her head again, so I helped her and wiped the tears with the edge of the sheet.

"Please don't cry, Mom. It will be alright."

"Talking with you makes me think that it could be. I see you caring for your little brother and you know how he looks up to you. You made me realize that I've been wrong to let your father hurt you. You convinced me that we do have enough. We have us."

I watched as the look of anguish started to leave Mom's face. Through a few last tears she even tried to smile. For the last few days, I was trying to stop her from dwelling on the past, when now it seemed she needed to resolve these feelings, once and for all. I realized that it was my being here that was giving her what she needed to feel at peace. I wish that Malcolm could hear her say how much this hurt her then and how much she loves us. We might not have had the best family life, but Mom always did the best she knew how. She never meant to hurt us. She was dealing with the same fears as we were.

I kissed her on the head and she tried so hard to smile again.

"Harry, I need to tell you something. I wish Malcolm could hear, but if you would, I need you to help me talk to him later. I don't want to wait."

"Sure, Mom, I will."

"When your father gets back, I'm going to tell him to leave. It's my house and I'll need to find a job, but it will work out somehow."

"If that's what will make you happy, Mom, of course I support you."

"I'm doing it for all of us, Harry. You convinced me that it's just not worth putting any of us through any more years of this, but most especially you boys."

Mom was still finding it hard to talk but it was easing her conscience, so she struggled to continue.

"I need you to help me with Malcolm more than ever," she said. "I need you to promise that you will watch out for him."

"I will, Mom. You know I will."

I always had back then, until he was older and pulled away from me. Mom spoke slowly, but I waited patiently, since it was making her feel good to tell me these things.

"I can do it then, Harry. I will tell him to pack when he comes home. I'll call the police station to tell them, should there be a problem. But he wouldn't dare take it further. We'll be alright," she said.

It was the first time in days that I saw my mother calm. Much like the way she looked the day my father died.

"I'm tired now, Harry. I'm going to get some sleep. We can talk more a little later."

I pulled the sheet up to her neck and sat on the bed looking at Mom. She wanted so badly to set her life right. It seemed that making these final amends with her past was what she needed. I couldn't help but cry when Mom began to breathe even shallower than before. I was staring at her and she smiled, and as I was looking she took her last breath.

"You rest, Mom," I said. I love you."

As it happened when I entered the room, I felt an intense vibration running through me, a blinding brightness, and I shuttered.

Everything around me was changing back, as did Mom. I looked down and saw my body as it was before, and I turned to look in the mirror behind me. Something powerful had touched us.

My head started to ache with a pressure so hard that I bent over and put my head to my knees. Pictures were exploding in my brain, memories I never had before. It felt as if each new thought was fighting for space inside. In my mind I saw a house, my house, but not the one we lived in when Sarah left me. Sarah was there, though, and I was hugging the girls as I went out. They were memories in reverse and speeding up, with worsening pain as they passed. It felt as if it would never stop, but it finally did when the memories reached that time in this room, twenty four years ago. But these were entirely new memories, and Mom had demanded that our father leave. My life had taken a different path.

New thoughts filled my mind of finishing school and going on to study for the certifications I always wanted. I worked in Manhattan and commuted on the train I watched so many times, crossing the Moodna Viaduct. I pictured Malcolm living close by and saw our children playing together. It was difficult to tell what was real anymore.

I held Mom's hand for a moment and then left the room. As I walked toward the stairs, I had flashes of seeing Malcolm, Julia and Brian downstairs with Sarah and my girls. I could picture them waiting in the sitting room. We were taking turns staying with Mom. My thoughts felt so foreign, but some were beginning to come into focus. The new memories were fighting to merge with the ones I'd known.

I stopped short of the entrance to the sitting room and listened for a moment. I heard the girls talking with their cousin Brian. I could hear Sarah complaining about some annoyance she went through at the market. I knew now that when I turned that corner, they would all be there. And yet when I entered, I was still speechless, and froze when I saw them. They could see in my face that I was disturbed. They were all staring at me, waiting for me to speak.

"Mom's gone," I said.

Kaela and Lainey came over and I bent down to hug them as we cried for Mom. Malcolm and Julia hugged with Brian between them. Sarah just looked on. I was sad about Mom, so it was easy to hide the shock of how my life had changed around me. There was nothing I could tell them they would believe. They would write it off as depression over Mom. I should be happy that Malcolm stayed close and my family was back together, but I was overwhelmed by what occurred.

Sarah came over to hug me, but it felt cold. I'd need time to adjust. I still felt resentment for her leaving me, in what I still most felt was my real life.

Malcolm walked over, coming so close that I almost jumped back. Then I noticed he had a look of sadness in his eyes that I hadn't seen since we were young. His face was no longer harsh and angry, but now looked soft.

Malcolm held the tops of my arms and said, "Harry. Was Mom comfortable when she died?"

I couldn't even answer before he placed his head in my chest and sobbed.

I whispered. "She was, little brother, she was. She loved you so much, Malcolm, and she asked me to watch out for you."

Malcolm looked up at me, face wet, unable to hold his mouth from pulling down and said, "You always have, Harry."

The way things changed, I had all the things I thought I ever wanted. But a part of me didn't know what I wanted anymore. For the next few minutes, all I needed to do was hug my girls again.

There was no reason for the kids to stay, so I told Sarah she should take Julia and the kids back to our house. Malcolm and I needed to make arrangements for Mom. We would meet them later.

Chapter 10

It was Thursday morning, the day of Mom's funeral. I was getting ready to go. I felt distracted as I dressed and between every action, I hesitated for a moment in thought. In the couple of days since Mom died, the last of the new memories had mostly settled in. Some of them were easy to place in the reality they had come from. With others it was not that easy. It was as if I had lived two lives from that time until now. It wasn't that I felt comfortable, but I accepted that I could never go back. I wondered if it was selfish to believe I might want to go back.

Malcolm was nothing like the person I visited just days ago in his home. In this world, Malcolm had been young enough to escape the worst of the damage. Even in the sadness of making arrangements for Mom, it was great to have my little brother back.

Malcolm and I had both struggled to get the money we needed to finish college, but we did finish and were both doing well. I had long since become the network engineer that I had been studying to be, and the firm I worked for in Manhattan paid me well. Sarah had her bigger home, and even though she didn't leave me, we had still drifted apart.

We needed to leave so Sarah took the girls to the car, while I still struggled with my tie. She couldn't help but look annoyed when I got in after making them wait. I thought she could have tried harder to hide it, considering what I was going through with my mother's death.

We arrived at the parking lot and saw some of Mom's friends drive in as well. I thought about how hard it was to get by after Mom threw our father out, but we were happy. When our father left, Mom took a job in a bakery to provide for us, and some of the people she baked for over the years were here to pay their respects.

It was still upsetting to me that such a big part of me died with my mother and I wanted to know how. So much of what I was came from the struggles in that past. That life gave me strength of character and a strong sense of empathy. My father being there had provided me with a sterling example of everything I should never be. I just didn't feel like me anymore, and I missed Lacie so much.

Once inside, Mom's friends and neighbors came to greet me. They shook my hand and told me how sorry they were. Some of them I knew and some only knew Mom. It was a fine service. I wrote a short tribute to Mom and when I got up to speak, the room grew silent. I spoke about her courage, love and compassion. I talked about how she truly loved Malcolm and me, our wives and her grandchildren; that she would have done anything for her family. Unable to hold a tear, one fell, and I took a moment to compose myself. I told them how, of all the selfless deeds that I ever witnessed, I'd seen the most from Mom. As I finished, I thanked her friends and neighbors for being a part of her life.

Malcolm and Julia invited their minister to speak. The room was silent as he stood for a moment looking at his notes. Now I knew how Malcolm turned to God. It was because of Julia's strong faith. I remembered how, at first, he told me he loved the sense of community, how it brought his family closer together. Later, he began to believe. We were always tolerant of each others views now, and we kept them to ourselves.

Their minister started to speak and he referred to Mom as if he knew her. He spoke in rote phrases, about how she was in a better place, and that someday we would all be together again in heaven. He said we needed to rejoice in her death. I was uncomfortable listening to this, but Malcolm and his family deserved to have their minister speak if it made them feel better.

In my new memories, once our father left, Malcolm came out of his shell. I watched over him to help Mom and he looked to me for guidance. He was my little buddy. When we were grown, I was thrilled when he married Julia. She's a kind person and when I'm with them, I can see how much they love each other. It was clear that this reality had profoundly changed Malcolm's life for the better and I was happy for that.

The service concluded and everyone began filing out for the drive to the cemetery. On the way, Sarah and I chose to take our car while Malcolm, Julia and Brian rode in the limousine. It became a long row of cars as we drove from the funeral home to the cemetery. Sarah never said a word. Mom had touched so many more lives now and I admired even more her strength as we were growing up. When our father left, he caused little trouble and we learned that he moved to a small one room in Sullivan County. It was near the yard where he started his trucking runs. He never tried to make amends and we never reached out to him. He died a lonely death.

At Mom's grave I said a few more words, as did Malcolm and his minister. Then they lowered Mom's casket into the ground. We provided a pile of carnations and I tossed the first one in and watched as everyone passed and did the same. At the end of the line, I saw Kaela and Lainey walking up to toss theirs in.

"I love you, Grandma Ladd," said Lainey.

She tossed in her flower and walked away. Then Kaela tossed in hers.

"I will miss you, Grandma," Kaela said.

She began to cry and I went over to pick her up. We both cried and I hugged her as I carried her to the car. Without the pressures of my father, Mom had been so much more a part of the girls' lives. I knew that Kaela finally understood she would never see her again.

The others walked quietly to their cars and drove off, but the limousine waited to take Malcolm and his family back to their car. When Kaela went to join Lainey and Brian, I hugged Malcolm and for a moment we felt like boys again.

"Mom was proud of you, little buddy," I told him.

"She was a good mother, wasn't she, big brother?" he asked.

"She always did the best she could," I said.

Malcolm and I just stared deeply at each other, both with a look as if we were thinking the same thought about Mom. Maybe we were. Then he broke the silence.

"Maybe you can bring Sarah and the kids over for the fourth of July?" Malcolm asked. "There's a small parade in our town and the girls might enjoy it."

I told him I would talk with Sarah and call him about it.

Sarah and Julia were talking and when Julia saw us walking their way, she came over to say goodbye.

"I'm sorry that we lost Mother, Harry," Julia said.

I kissed her on the cheek and thanked her.

"Brian, be good for your mom and dad," I said.

"I will, Uncle Harry," he told me.

Julia and Malcolm hugged the girls and we left.

Driving home I hardly spoke. When Malcolm talked about the Fourth, it reminded me about Billy, and the concert I would have taken him to on the Sunday before. But now he no longer knew me. It made me think again about Lacie and how much I missed her. But now she never met me. I knew that life was better for most of us now, but I still missed the people in that neighborhood, my friends.

Driving past town on the way home was stranger than I imagined it would be. I saw Brice outside setting up his tables and when I looked up above the computer store, I saw a "For Rent" sign in the apartment window. As tough as it was when Sarah left me in my other memories, I had grown to love that town and the people.

When we got back to our house, Sarah went on as usual, concerned with the girls and the things she enjoyed. We had grown more distant in both realities, but in this one, I was successful and easygoing enough that she hadn't left me. Sarah had what she wanted: a comfortable car, matching outfits for the girls and a home sufficient for her ambitions. What was somehow overlooked was her passion for me and I had been satisfied enough with the love of my children.

I went straight to my workshop in the garage. There was a tall, four-foot-wide wooden shelf unit filled with books, many of them on the sciences. I felt obsessed with finding anything that could shed some light on what brought me here, any clue. There had to be some possible, physical reason. I would never accept it to be an act of a god.

I was thumbing through my books when Lainey peeked through the shop door, and then came in to hug me. She handed me a little piece of paper with a hand-drawn woman on it.

"I drew a picture of Grandma Ladd for you, Daddy," she said.

"Thank you, sweetheart," I told her.

The drawing was of a woman, with mountains and a couple of trees drawn in the background.

"It's Grandma at Black Rock," she said.

Unlike when Mom brought Malcolm and me as kids, she started to have trouble climbing the hills as she got older. But she took the girls there anyway, and just stayed on the road that led to the lake.

"Daddy, Mommy told me I can still go to camp next week."

"Of course you can, Lainey. I want both of you to go," I said. "Your mom bought all your outfits and the other supplies you need. You two will really enjoy it."

Lainey picked up the picture she drew and looked at it once more.

"Thanks, Dad. This picture is not your Fathers Day present, you know. Kaela and I are bringing them home tomorrow when school ends."

"I can't wait," I said. "I know I'll love them."

Lainey went back upstairs and I began to search through my books and browse the web. I was looking for relevant theories for how this change could have possibly occurred. I had a feeling that at some time in the past, I read about a field in physics that might provide at least a clue. I just couldn't pin it down. But as I read into the night, a slight chill made me shiver. It reminded me of what happened in Mom's room the day she died. How I felt my entire body vibrating, going in and out of the event.

There was something about "String Theory" I thought.

I dug for the books I had on the subject and as I read I started to remember what it was about.

According to string theory, all matter and all forces exist because of tiny vibrating one-dimensional strings. The vibrations of the pattern were what gave matter and the forces its properties. It was much like the different length of the strings of a piano and how it changes the frequencies, creating the different tones. All that exists might just be notes in an amazing cosmological symphony. In addition, when taken the next step into M theory, it opens up the possibility that our universe could be one membrane among an infinite number of others; infinite parallel universes existing side by side.

I found a transcript online from a PBS Nova show, "The Elegant Universe," where scientist and author, Brian Greene said:

"And there's no reason to be disappointed with one particular outcome or another, because quantum mechanics suggests that each of the possibilities, like getting a yellow juice or a red juice, may actually happen. They just happen to happen in universes that are parallel to ours, universes that seem as real to their inhabitants as our universe seems to us."

Two membranes may have touched, producing a bubble in the room, slightly offset, and merging the past with present. I felt then that I may have gotten as close to an answer as I would ever get. Whatever the cause, what was certain was that an opportunity became available for Mom to alter that past. And she took it. Being enveloped in the event must have been why I still retained my old memories.

I was getting tired, but continued to avoid being around Sarah as I had since Mom died. I had been purposely falling asleep on the couch downstairs. I'm sure she attributed it to the loss of Mom but it was more than that. I didn't want to be with Sarah anymore.

Because Mom was ill, I had taken the week off from my job in Manhattan, but on Monday I'd be going back. The kids would be at camp when I got home, so I decided I would talk with Sarah then. I wanted to move out as soon as possible. I was certain the girls would be OK, since they were when Sarah left me before. Now at least I could afford a better apartment, one with an extra bedroom for the girls when they stayed. Just the same, they'd be close.

I was able to remain reclusive through the weekend, even on Father's Day. Sarah didn't give me a card, but suggested I take them all out for dinner. I told her I just wasn't up to it. On Monday, I went off to work and Sarah brought the girls to camp. I was comfortable with where I work now, and I love my position. I appreciated that my coworkers and manager were supportive throughout Mom's illness. I was staging several projects, and I had so many electronic devices around my office that I felt like a boy in a toy store.

On the commute home, I stared out the train window at the beautiful ponds and streams. Just before my station, there was a ride over the long and high trestle stretching over the Moodna Valley just below. From up high, there was also a great view of Black Rock Forest in the distance. This train to me had been an object of curiosity for so long. I often wondered about the people aboard.

When I got home, it was just after six o'clock and Sarah was out front watering the flowers that surrounded the porch. I sat on the steps and asked how it went today with dropping the girls off at camp. She told me how excited they were when they arrived and how Kaela kept her sister close to her. I told Sarah I appreciated the way she cared for the girls. I then told her I needed to talk with her.

I explained that I was truly sorry, but I just couldn't stay with her anymore. I was as kind as I could be about my reasoning and assured Sarah that I would still take care of the house and bills. She wouldn't have to worry about those things. It was important to me that my girls be affected as little as possible.

Sarah knew why we should split up and I saw no look of surprise. She never mentioned counseling because she too knew it wouldn't help. We would determine visiting arrangements once I found a place and settled in, the legal arrangements as well. Sarah and I agreed that we should talk to the girls together when they came back from camp.

I spent the night packing many of my things into boxes and stored them in the garage. At least now I would be able to afford an apartment that would fit my things and still give the girls their private bedroom. I packed up my shop, except this time I had a few better tools. I would need room for my bookshelf now with my respectable amount of books. When I felt I'd packed enough for one night, I got ready for bed and went to sleep on the couch. It had gotten late.

I brought the classifieds to work with me the next day and arranged to look at a couple of two bedroom apartments that evening. They were down near Sarah Wells Trail just past town. When I arrived at the train station after work, I put the paper with the circled ads on the passenger seat and drove down Route 94 toward town. The light at Route 208 turned red and, as I waited, I looked into the computer repair shop and saw Hewitt sorting items in his front display window. Looking up I saw the "For Rent" sign again in the window above his store and felt compelled to turn around. I parked in front and went inside. Hewitt walked back to the counter believing I needed a computer part.

"What can I get for you?" he asked.

"My name is Harry," I said. "Would you mind if I took a look at the apartment you have for rent?"

"Sure, give me a moment and I'll get the keys. I'm Hewitt. It's nice to meet you, Harry."

He took out the keys and turned the sign around on the glass door. It read "Be Back In" and had a little round face showing minutes which he set to fifteen. He locked the front door behind us and we walked up the stairs to the apartment. It was empty, but it made me think of those few nights with Lacie and made me feel at home. Although I could afford a better place, I had the money to fix this one up. I could learn to deal with a living room full of my objects for now, but there was only one thing else I would need.

"Hewitt, I would like to rent it, but there is one thing I could really use," I told him.

He seemed interested to hear.

"I noticed the outline of a door behind the entrance and that the door was moved to the hall. Is that room large enough to make into a bedroom?" I asked. "I would like an extra room for when my girls stay. It looks like the door to that room could easily be moved back into this apartment."

"That was a bedroom," he said. "I converted it for storage when the apartment went unoccupied for so long. I can move the storage to the basement and have the work done in a few days."

I already knew it was large enough and he was happy to add it for a slight increase. When we settled on an amount, I wrote him a check and he told me he would like to explain a few things. Hewitt led me out back and showed me the dumpster where I could throw my trash. He told me how if Brooks Tavern had a good night there may not be parking in front, and showed me a space in the back where I could park.

"Ben owns the deli there. Just don't park in his spot," he said.

I told him I would remember and when I looked over at the back of Ben's place, I saw some boxes of clothes and other items. I recognized a few of the objects, but most especially Billy's ham radio, placed on top of one of the garbage containers.

"What's that?" I asked Hewitt, as I pointed to the radio.

"It's broken," he said. "It belonged to a vet who used to live in the apartment over the deli."

"Used to live?" I asked. "Where did he go?"

"He died last week. He was depressed and committed suicide down by Moodna creek. I felt bad because it started when that damn thing broke. He asked if he could sweep up for me each day in trade for a repair. A guy with an artificial leg and he offered to sweep up. I told him I couldn't help him, though. I only fix computers. He couldn't afford the price that the repair shop quoted him."

"I'm sorry," I said.

Hewitt would never realize how really sorry I was. Billy lost the chance to be with his friends on the radio when I wasn't there to help him. It was all that he had.

I thanked Hewitt and he gave me a set of keys.

For the rest of the week and through the weekend it was multiple trips to the home improvement stores, then spackling, sanding and painting. Hewitt had the door moved and I was finished painting the last of the trim. The final thing to do was to change the kitchen and bathroom faucets. It would still be crowded, but it had the extra bedroom for the girls. With a little bit of money now, it had really come together.

I finished all the work by three o'clock on Sunday afternoon so I went down to the deli to get a sandwich. Ben was coming out of the walk-in refrigerator with his hands full of meats for the refrigerated counter case where he stored them.

"Be right with you," he said.

After he put the meats in the case, he asked me what I would like, then he started to make my sandwich.

"My name is Harry," I told him. "I rented the apartment above Hewitt's shop."

"Oh, you're the guy who Hewitt told me was fixing the whole place up."

"Just trying to give it a few improvements," I said.

"I'm Ben. Glad to meet you," he said.

Ben was such a nice guy. He talked about things I already remembered about him but I acted as if I heard them for the first time. I told him about my girls and how I had split from Sarah. He said he was sorry it didn't work out and I thanked him for that. I noticed the large broken clock on the wall over the tables and remembered how easy it was to repair.

"I see your clock is broken and I enjoy repairing things," I told him. "I have a little time. Do you mind if I take a quick look at that?"

"That's very nice of you," Ben said. "I'd given up on it."

I asked if he had any tools, so he handed me the small toolbox that he kept behind the counter. Since I already repaired this before, it took me just a few minutes to do it again. I set the correct time again and watched as it moved to the next minute.

"I always loved that clock," he said. "Thank you, Harry. Please, the sandwich is on me."

I thanked him and sat down at the first table to eat. I saw Belita come in and she went up to Ben at the counter. I wanted to say hello to her because I knew her well, but I remembered not to. When he started to slice her cold cuts, he couldn't wait to point out the fact that his clock was working again.

"Belita, this is Harry. He's renting the apartment above Hewitt's place. He just fixed my clock."

"Pleased to meet you, Harry," Belita said. "I wish you knew something about blenders."

"Well, actually I do," I told her. "I should have all my things in by Friday and I'll have my tools then. After that, you can drop it off and I'll take a look at it."

"Thank you, Harry, I will," she said. "I was holding onto it until I put enough money aside to have it fixed. Maybe you would charge me less?" she asked.

"I won't charge you at all. It's a hobby of mine," I said.

"Can't I pay you something?" she asked.

I thought for a moment.

"Well, if you bake pies, maybe you can bake me an apple pie."

Of course I knew she did.

"I make them all the time. I would be happy to," she said. "Thank you."

I remembered exactly what I did to fix her blender as well, so that would be an exercise just as the clock was. I thanked Ben for the sandwich and told them both that I would see them again.

Hewitt was going to help me this week by letting the delivery people in when they brought my furniture. I planned to take a few loads of boxes each night and then stop in Brooks Tavern for a beer. On Monday night when I did, it was nice to hear Brice tell his stories again. When I told him what apartment I had taken, he let me know that Ben bragged about me when they spoke.

"You made quite an impression," Brice said. "He's so happy about that clock."

"It was really nothing," I told him. "I was happy I could help."

Brice talked about Lacie and the more he did, the more I missed her. On the weekdays, Brice had more time for conversation. There wasn't the crowd he often had on the weekends, just a modest amount of customers tonight and the regulars at the bar. It was amusing to meet the regulars again for the first time. After a couple beers, I had to go get some sleep before work, so I said good night and left.

I called Sarah from work Tuesday morning and told her I'd have the last of my boxes out on Friday, but I would see her again on Sunday. We were going to talk to the girls when we picked them up at camp. My girls mean so much to me, but I could never stay with Sarah now. I knew they'd be fine and I would be living just down the road. For the next three evenings, I brought over boxes and unpacked most everything. With my new things, the living room area was even more crowded than I imagined, but it would do. Tomorrow, I planned to bring over the last of my things and stay.

I stopped at Brooks Tavern and, when I told Brice I was finally moving in tomorrow, he told me to come have dinner on him as a welcome to the neighborhood. I thanked him and said that, if he ever had anything broken, he should tell me first. He laughed a little and then reminded me of the time. I lost track while we were talking and he knew I had to get some sleep before work. I really like Brice. He is everything a father should be.

When Friday came, I felt a sense of relief. After, work I went to pick up the last of my boxes and then stopped for some groceries. When the last of my boxes were unpacked, I made my first pot of coffee here. I had missed having coffee by this window, putting a soundtrack to the goings-on below. Friday evening was a little busier in town and again I had my view from above. I watched as people walked up the block. Some would walk through town. Some went to the basement jazz bar and others to Brooks.

When I took my eyes down from a sip, I saw Lacie walk out by the tables, clearing one for a couple. Boy, it was great to see her again. I really missed her, so I thought I would at least stop in to be closer. Brice was expecting to treat me to dinner anyway, so I washed up and walked over.

When I entered, it was hard for me to keep my eyes off of Lacie. I sat down at the end of the bar and caught glimpses of her as she walked by. It was busier tonight so it took a few minutes for Brice to come over with a beer, but when he did, he reminded me that dinner was on him. He looked around for a moment and when he saw Lacie he called.

"Lacie, please come here for a moment. That's my daughter, who I spoke about," he told me.

She walked over and I could feel my gut sink. She looked beautiful to me: tight jeans, a soft shirt, and clean white apron. I needed it to seem as if we just met, but it was difficult.

"Yes, Dad?" she asked.

"Lacie, I'd like you to meet Harry," Brice said. "He just moved into the apartment above Hewitt's store and I promised him dinner on us."

"Nice to meet you, Harry," she said. "Come and sit in a booth. I'll bring you a menu."

"Thanks Lacie, I will. I won't need a menu. I would like the roasted boneless chicken," I said.

"I will go back and ask him to make it fresh for you," she said.

When she came out of the kitchen, she brought some food to another booth and then came over.

"Do you mind if I sit with you and talk?" she asked.

"Not at all, I would like that."

We talked, and between serving tables she came back to talk some more. She didn't know how much I loved her. I knew what she liked to talk about and so many things about her. I hoped it would be the advantage I needed to make her fall in love with me again. We talked for quite a while, but as much as I wanted to stay, I knew I shouldn't. I didn't want to rush things and there were so many matters to settle. When I finished the chicken, Lacie was checking the tables outside and I went to the bar to thank Brice for the dinner. She noticed that I was leaving and came over to the bar. Lacie gently grabbed my arm and when she looked at me, I saw something in her eyes.

"I enjoyed talking with you Harry. Maybe we can talk again."

"I would like that," I told her.

978-0-595-47029-7
0-595-47029-7

Printed in Great Britain
by Amazon.co.uk, Ltd.,
Marston Gate.